I0637532

RIDING THE SHIFTER SHADOWS PAPERBACK

An Enemies to Lovers Paranormal Romance

COLBIE CLARKE

BYTESPRESS
PUBLISHING
BRING YOURS TO YOUR PAGE

BYTES PRESS

CONTENTS

CHAPTER ONE

Eris

• • • • • • • • • •

I T'S STARTING TO RAIN. I'm sure I felt a drop a second ago. And there's another. I look up, scanning the patch of billowy clouds visible between the tall office buildings comprising the central hub's business and entertainment district. My attention is drawn to the striking geometric shape of the Museum building looming high before me. The simplicity and clean lines of this structure have a calming effect on me, and I turn back to the street, certain the rain will hold off for a few minutes more.

I've been standing here for fifteen minutes waiting for him. Scott, I think his name is. I'll give him another five, max, then I'm going in without him. Heaven save me from blind dates.

My coworker, Ben, set me up and I regret agreeing to it. According to Ben, Scott is smart and handsome and has a great job within the Authority as a Registrant for the Mage Commission. Not that his work status matters to me. I work Intelligence for the Global Cabal, so technically, I outrank him. God, maybe he's intimidated by my status and is not coming! Men can be funny about that sort of thing.

A car pulls up right in front of me and parks. It's a nice car. Black and sleek. Probably one of the latest models. I guess they're paying Registrants well these days. The driver's side opens, and a gorgeous man steps out. Tanned with dark hair gelled and styled into place. He's wearing a button-down shirt matched with a pair of light-colored slacks that make him look dressed up but casual. He turns to the entrance where I'm standing, then smiles the moment our eyes connect.

Oh, I hope this is him. He looks polished and well-kept, like a guy who hangs all his clothes up and doesn't possess a single pair of jeans. He's walking straight for me. Looks like I might've hit the jackpot.

"Eris?" he asks when he's about a foot away.

I smile and nod. "And you must be Scott, right?" I close the gap between us and shake his hand.

He smiles back, his eyes briefly drifting over me. He looks about as relieved as I feel.

"I gotta tell you, it's nice to meet you. Ben wasn't kidding when he told me you are a knock-out." He laughs and continues to give me a solid once-over. Since I'm eyeballing him the same way, I can't complain about the knock-out crack.

I'm wearing my blue midi dress with matching pumps. It's got a cleavage but nothing too suggestive. I didn't want to appear too dressy or too eager. I also think the outfit looks mousy for this date. Apparently, not, though. Scott seems pleased with how I look.

"You look beautiful."

"Thanks," I say. "You look good, yourself."

"Appreciate the compliment. I spent about an hour coming up with this look only to realize it's really just business casual."

We laugh at the small joke, and he touches my elbow, nudging me along toward the glass wall of doors fronting the museum entrance.

He's funny, too. Nice. I'm beginning to forgive his late arrival.

The signs leading to the big exhibit are overwhelming. I would have liked to appreciate the beauty of the museum's foyer, however, the hype over this exhibit has been all the rage in the Central Hub for months now. Every few years, the Scepter of Magnus Circadia makes the rounds to all the museums, and I always seem to miss it. Not this time, though.

"I've been looking forward to finally seeing the scepter," I tell Scott. "Have you ever been to this exhibit before?"

He shakes his head. "No, I never had the chance to see it."

"Me neither. Every single time it comes to town, something comes up. This date came right on time."

He nods and I catch him stealing a glance at my cleavage. Maybe the dress is more revealing than I thought.

We walk casually through the museum, stopping a couple of times to admire an exhibit along the way. There is a line waiting to enter the room where the scepter is being exhibited. As we join the que, we are treated to pictures of the scepter, all blown up on displays lining our path to the entrance.

Scott picks up a brochure and reads out loud as we shuffle closer to the door. *"At one point in time, the Scepter of Magnus Circadia was known to possess the power to destroy or displace entire cities. Mage scientists have been studying the scepter for years, hoping to learn how to access its full power. To date, the scientists have been unsuccessful, only scratching the surface of the scepter's capabilities."* He frowns and says, "Wow. Sounds like quite a weapon. Hard to believe it's sitting in a museum and not under lock and key to keep the public safe."

"Oh, we'll be perfectly safe. For one thing, no one's ever been able to figure out how to get it to work. The best guess anyone has is that it was attuned only to Circadia. And since he's long dead..." I shrug.

He smiles. "You really do have a big interest in this thing, huh?"

"I like history. Especially about the war. Part of it has to do with my job, but Circadia and his scepter have always held a special interest for me."

"Huh. Yeah, Ben said that you work in Intelligence."

My stomach tightens, but I keep my smile up. "Yeah. For the GC for about three years. They hired me straight out of school."

"Wow," he says. "You must be pretty smart. I know guys who have tried their whole careers to get into the GCI."

I can feel my face flushing. I'm not one who brags about my accomplishments. I'm glad he doesn't seem threatened, though. "I guess they saw something in me that they wanted, you know?"

The line is moving again, and he puts the brochure on a table. As we walk forward, he smiles down at me and slips his hand into mine. It feels good. Protective even.

We make it through the doorway, the last two in, before they close the gates again. I had heard only small groups were allowed to see the exhibit. The large room has a myriad of related displays. Items from the war, such as mage robes and pieces from buildings long destroyed. By each display is a metal plaque detailing where the item came from and the history behind it.

"Huh," he says as we look around for a moment. "I don't think I see it."

I smile up at him. "It's not in here." I point to a marked door with velvet ropes in front of it. "It's there under guard."

He raises his eyebrows and nods. "Well, we came all this way to see it. Let's go and see it."

"Don't you want to check out any of the other displays? I mean, the history behind how Magnus won us the war is really fascinating."

"Yeah, but I kind of want to see the goods. You know what I mean?"

He chuckles and I join him. "You're the kind of guy who likes dessert first, huh?"

"You caught me," he says as he sticks his arm out to me. "Shall we?"

I loop my arm in his and we walk together to the ropes.

The guard standing next to the entrance looks us over and says, "No flash photography allowed under penalty of the authority." To emphasize his point, he points to a sign saying just that and several other rules, such as "No Touching of the display glass."

I sneer at the guard, rejecting his assumption that we need to be told how to behave as if we're children.

"Yes, sir," says Scott smartly and I nudge him for his irreverence.

The guard gives us both a narrowed-eye stare as we walk past him into the room and devolve into giggles.

The room is dark. Almost pitch, even. No windows or outdoor light from any angle. In fact, the only light is a spotlight shining down from the ceiling and casting an amber glow on a large display case. It feels empty and as we walk toward the display, it becomes apparent we are the only people in the room.

"Ohhh!" I gasp as we approach the display. The beauty of the shining silver scepter levitating in the center of the case pulls at my heart. I feel an ache in the pit of my stomach as I come close.

"Holy shit. That's it, huh?"

Scott appears as underwhelmed by the display as I am overwhelmed. I'm rendered speechless as I stand before the scepter. I've seen hundreds of photos of it on the net, but no picture can do justice to the depth and exquisite, pulsing energy of the real scepter.

I study it, my eyes memorizing every inch, leaning in as close as possible to get the best view. I see swirled engravings carved into the handle. Not random, a pattern with meaning, likely runes imbuing the base metal with power. The solid gold staff is fused with silver which fills the carved runes. Two precious metals, known to be porous receptors for mage power, are masterfully merged to create the staff, topped with a clear crystal. The gem, held in the embrace of a gold filigree setting to connect it to the staff, is glossed into a high shine, making it appear translucent in this light.

I've stopped moving and am uncertain how long my feet have been frozen to the floor. My vision is eclipsed by the scepter. It is the most beautiful creation I've ever seen in my life.

"It's beautiful," I whisper. I feel Scott behind me, his arms sliding around my waist.

"Not as beautiful as you," he says softly.

I feel him nuzzle my neck, his lips touching my skin. His kiss pulls me out of my revelry, and I flinch away from him, pushing his hands from around my waist.

"Moving fast, aren't you?" I say with a nervous chuckle.

"I don't know. Being here with you alone in the dark does something to me."

"We aren't exactly alone, Scott. There's a guard outside that door waiting for us to leave so that he can let in the next viewers."

Yes, well, while you've been standing entranced, I went back and locked the door from the inside. Nice of their security to have an old-fashioned deadbolt in place. We won't be disturbed."

I blink at him. God, we haven't even said two words to one another. "I don't think so, Scott. Let's go check out the rest of the displays, okay?" I turn to walk away, but he grabs my arm and spins me back to face him.

"I have zero interest in anything in this ridiculous museum—except for you." His voice is low and filled with malice as he pulls me to him "I'm just following your lead, beautiful."

Alarms are going off in my mind. Following my lead? What the hell does that even mean? Does he think I gave him some kind of signal? I need to get out of here.

"Listen," I say as I put my hands on his chest to push him away. "I don't know what you think is going on here—"

He tightens his embrace, locking his arms around me so I can't escape. "Come on, baby. Stop playing around. You know you want it as much as I do. All you uptight career hussies are just waiting for a real man to show you what you've been missing."

He leans in to kiss me and suddenly I'm terrified. I struggle in his arms, and move my head back and away. His teeth draw blood from my lips as I lean my weight back on one leg and leverage the movement to kick my knee up, but I miss the target between his legs and succeed only in pushing him back a step.

Despite my resistance, he holds me firm, smiling, as he lifts me off my feet and carries me into a dark corner of the room.

I catch my breath and let out a scream for help while continuing to struggle against his superior strength.

There's a low hissing somewhere in the room. It's a sound I know well, one we all know well. It's the sound of a portal opening. Or, at least, that's what I think it is. I can't imagine who would be opening a portal in this room.

He slams me against the wall, and places a hand over my mouth and nose, cutting off my air.

"I like a woman with a fight in her," His laugh is maniacal as he reaches up my dress and claws at my underwear. "Makes it all the sweeter, if you know what I mean?" His hand busy elsewhere, I scream again, but he rams my head hard into the wall.

I see stars as pain shoots through my head. He's hiking up my skirt now, trying to pull down my underwear. I struggle, but he's moved himself between my legs, pressing me against the wall. I'm praying that the guard has heard something. That anyone has heard something. Please, somebody, come in here. Please...

He moves his hand off my mouth and forces another kiss.

I bite him and he yells out, yanking away from me, fingers touching his bloodied lip. "Oh," he says with a laugh. "You are going to pay for—"

He's knocked away from me, so fast, that for a moment, I stand silently, too stunned to move. In the dim light, I watch him slide on his side across the floor, skidding to a stop near the door.

"Are you okay?" a deep voice asks me.

I look away from Steve's motionless body to see, standing in front of me, a rough-looking man with long dark hair tied back in a ponytail. His face is in shadow, but his eyes glisten. My own eyes are playing tricks on me, as I think I see a flash of red before he blinks and I look away. He's wearing a leather kutte with patches on it and a pair of distressed blue jeans. A biker?

I can't speak, can't pull a coherent thought out of my head to verbalize it. And if I could, all I have are questions. What's a biker doing here? Where did he come from? How did he get past the guard?

He reaches out to me and I flinch, side-stepping slightly away from him.

He stops short of touching me and a slight smile turns up the corners of his mouth. "I'm not going to hurt you, Princess," he says. His hand moves again and touches my shoulder lightly. In the tussle with Scott, my dress slipped down off my shoulders. He takes the fabric and pulls it back into place.

I feel safe suddenly. The feeling pushes through my fear and washes over me when I look into his dark eyes. Who is this man…?

Before I can say thank you or ask one of the many questions running through my head, Scott groans loudly. "Shit...what the hell happened?"

We both turn toward him as he sits up. He's stunned, still, from being knocked across the room and holds his head, then looks up at us. The confusion on his face is apparent even across the dimly lit room as he squints and rapidly blinks bleary eyes.

A low, animal growl draws my attention back to the stranger. As he bares his teeth, I see fangs. A wolf shifter! Fear and excitement war inside of me. I've never seen one before up close.

I hear Scott emit an oddly high-pitched and surprisingly quiet scream and realize he's recognized the stranger as a shifter, too. He butt-walks backward, scurrying toward the flimsy shelter offered by a small exhibit case. Still seated on the floor, he stares at the stranger standing close to me. A second later, a large, dark stain appears in the front of his pants.

"Oh, this is just great." Someone says from behind the stranger. A younger, shorter man emerges from the open portal just as it dims and closes behind him. He is wearing the same biker-style clothes with the addition of a patch-filled ball cap riding high on his head. He pulls bulky gloves onto his hands. The gloves are odd. They have the look of heavy-duty electrician's gloves and there are wires coiled around the wrist cuffs leading to a small digital panel embedded in the cuff. "We don't have time for this."

The big shifter looks at me for a moment, then back to Scott. "Hurry up," he says to the man behind him. "I've got this."

I watch as the younger man adjusts some sort of control on the cuff of each glove, then proceeds to slide his hands through the protective glass of the display case. Obviously, these are not ordinary gloves. He takes hold of the scepter and withdraws his hands but stops when the scepter doesn't penetrate the glass. "Uh-oh."

As the shifter turns to look at his partner, Scott attempts a blindside attack. He lunges and rams his shoulder into the much larger shifter. Caught off guard, the shifter is pushed back and both of them crash into the scepter's display case.

The second man, gloved hands still inside the case, stumbles back as the glass shatters and the remnants of the case fall, settling into a mound of glass and debris on the floor, still spotlit by the cone of amber light illuminating the space now void of the scepter.

Scott and the shifter continue to grapple. The element of surprise in Scott's favor dwindles as the much larger shifter regains his footing. With a twist of his body, he brings his arms up and around Scott's neck, squeezing him tight.

"No! Stop!" I yell, but it's too late. I hear a sickening crunch as Scott's neck breaks and his body goes limp. The shifter releases him, and he falls to the floor in a heap.

I hear yelling from outside and so does the second man. He runs to the door, and, with a wave of his hand, a glow appears around it. I recognize a sealing spell and know that nobody is coming through that door without a mage to release the lock.

"Time to go," says the younger man. He holds the scepter up before stowing it in a drawstring backpack and slinging it across his back.

The shifter nods and steps over Scott's body, and then with a wave of his hand, a portal appears before him. It flickers as if it's about to close even before it's fully open. He looks confused and he and his partner exchange glances for a second. His partner doesn't waste any more time, though. He jumps through first, then the larger man follows, daring a glance back at me as if to see if I'm okay.

And they're gone. I don't know what the hell I just witnessed. I stand there stunned for a moment, then I see something glinting next to Scott's body. I walk over and pick it up. It's a necklace. On the end is a piece of polished amber...with a silver bullet in it.

As soon as the portal is fully gone, the door loses its seal and guards break it down. The guard who let us in runs up to me and then stops.

I'm kneeling next to Scott's body, glass is everywhere, and the scepter is gone. "Call an ambulance," I tell him, trying to keep the panic out of my voice.

CHAPTER TWO

Mac

• • • • • • • • • •

S OME MIGHT SAY THE whole thing went balls up. A few things we weren't expecting happened, but chaos aside, a win is a win. As the portal closes behind me, I'm thankful that we only ran into a couple of normie patrons instead of there being Authority cops there to greet us. Not sure if we could have escaped as easily if we had to shoot it out with them.

All that said, though, what happened wasn't exactly a good situation either.

We knew there might be patrons, but we only really planned for human ones because of the museum's location. Humans are easy to handle because most of them never leave the central hub. They're prissy, soft-handed people who are afraid of their own shadows. They see somebody like me and run the other way. The plan was, if there were any patrons, we'd intimidate them into silence until we could get the scepter and portal out.

Of course, who could expect we'd arrive in the middle of an assault? As soon as I opened the portal, I saw the woman being held against her will. She was fighting hard but had no chance of getting away. He was too determined and too strong.

I reacted on instinct, knocking the guy off her with a punch to his head. OK, so maybe I hit harder than necessary. It was pretty funny, though, watching him skid across that floor.

The woman must have been terrified. Looking at her leaning against the wall with only half her dress on, mascara running down her cheeks, blackening chestnut-colored skin, and nursing a bloodied lip, was a guarantee to jam my protector instinct into high gear.

She was a pretty thing. I wanted to grab her long, curly hair to pull back her head and gently lick her face clean. I hated to leave her, even though I left the sniveling coward who attacked for dead. There was no telling what that asshole did before I got there. Seeing her that way instantly pissed me off.

But then I had to fight the guy attacking her. I must have shorted something out with my energy levels during the fight. Getting that portal open was tougher than usual. My hands are still tingling from it. I probably need to get some sleep. I haven't had a good night's sleep in...I don't actually know.

A knock on the door rouses me from thought. Flip walks in with the scepter in hand. The meeting room is long and I'm at the far end, but he comes all the way over before sitting in one of the chairs near me and puts the scepter in front of me on the meeting table. He slumps down, exhaustion in his face and body language. "That almost went south, Pres. It's been a while since I've tried doing magic, you know? Kind of winded me."

"It went fine," I say to him. "The mission was to get the scepter and we got it. Nothing else matters."

Flip snorts, emptying the backpack contents onto the table and picking up one of the gloves to examine it.

"I thought you said those things would work." I know how much time he spent on making those damn things. Flip has got to be the smartest dumb guy I've ever known.

"Yeah. They did work." Flip says bitterly. "I guess I never took into account how the scepter itself would pass through the glass. "Anyway, turns out we didn't need it anyway, thanks to the normie."

I don't respond. I could use a drink. Making portals takes a lot out of a guy, especially this time. I'll never know how Dire was able to do them so easily.

"So, what now?" asks Flip.

"Now, how about you go grab us both a beer? I need a couple of minutes to think."

He nods. "Be right back." he agrees and heads back the way he came in.

I reach over to pick up the scepter from the table and lift it. The gold and silver glint as I hold it up to the shafts of light coming through the room's high windows. This thing is what let the mages win the war...and it's probably what led to or maybe caused my parent's death.

I wish I knew for sure what happened to them. All I do know comes from a few scribbles I found in my brother Biz's journal. Ever since I found his notebook, I've been trying to figure out what he knew about our parent's death. Pretty sure Biz knew what happened to them, but for some reason, he never spoke about it and everything in the journal is in code. It's taken me years to cipher enough to realize he knew what killed our parents. All I have are pieces...breadcrumbs that he left for me to follow.

Flip plops two cold bottles down on the table and I realize there are no answers to be had right now. Handing the scepter to Flip, I say, "Put it in the safe. I need to do some research before I move on to whatever's next."

Flip nods as he takes it to the safe in the corner of the room. "This has got to cost some serious change."

"I suppose it might, yeah."

After locking it in the safe, he stood up, hands on his hips, and asked, "How much do you think we'll get for it?"

I don't respond. I'm scowling at the back of his head.

"It's a national treasure," I say.

He turns to face me and as soon as he sees a scowl across my face, he pauses, smile drops. "Wha'd I say?"

"It's not a trinket we lifted off some rich central hub normie. Everybody in the city will be looking for it. We can't exactly unload it at a pawn shop, dumbass."

"I know that. But there's got to be a buyer, right? Some fancy art dealer somewhere?"

I sigh. "Not for this, Flip. And even there was, we're not selling."

He blinked for a moment in confusion. Then, "Okay, so why'd we steal something we can't sell?"

"I've got other more important uses for it. Go on and let everybody know we're back. And have Misty get me another beer, will you?"

"Right away," he says, walking out of the room.

I sit down at the head of the table. This chair has become my place since Dire, my best friend and former leader of our club, left to follow his heart. I'm not mad at him for going. Guys like us don't really get to fall in love. Not in any healthy way, anyway. I think about all the girls who have come through here looking for the bad boy life and washed out in one way or another and I'm happy he managed to find his soulmate. Good for him.

But with him gone, this has become my show and it hasn't exactly been easy. A few of the others felt differently about him leaving and I can't say that I blame them. Change is hard to accept even when everybody likes you. They came around eventually and fell in line. I mean, they had to. Nobody's stupid enough to try and challenge me for this chair.

All things considered, though, so far, things are going pretty good. We're in another location, still near the border, but far enough away so that we're not so easily found by wandering patrols. We're as organized as ever. We're whole and everybody's eating. That's how it should be.

I guess since we're relatively comfortable right now, that's why I've turned my energy to finding out who took out my folks. When Biz died, I was lost for a while. When you lose your whole family to a war that you didn't even start, you get bitter and hard. If I hadn't found this, I'd probably be just as dead as they are. Pope taking me in and putting my talents to work got me on the right track. I'd been so busy with club business and helping with the resistance that, for a while, I forgot about Biz's journal.

But ever since I figured out what he was trying to say, I've been waiting to be able to make moves. Magnus Circadia's scepter coming to town at a time when we don't have any immediate duties with Lillian and the resistance couldn't have been better timing. Now, the first step to solving this once and for all was done.

The door opens and Misty comes walking in. She used to run with Lillian and the resistance but at some point after Dire left, she asked to prospect for us. She was a tough little thing and wily. I always thought she'd make a good Maztec. She asked and we agreed and now she walks around wearing a kutte with *Prospect* patches on it.

She walks a cold beer over to me. "Hey, Mac," she says, a smart-alecky smile on her face. "Flip said you wanted a beer?"

I take it from her. "I told you about that. As long as you're prospecting, you don't get to address me directly."

She rolls her eyes. "Right, right," she says. "*Just because Dire liked me, that doesn't mean I'm automatically in. I gotta go through the same process as every other prospect.* I remember, boss."

"Yeah, sure you do. Don't pull that shit in front of the club, okay? I don't want to have to show you some respect in public."

Her smile faltered. Misty was sassy, but she wasn't a fool. "Yes, sir," she says, then, "So, you and Flip just get back?"

I sigh. It's like one ear and out the other. "We did."

She pauses, biting her lip anxiously. "Did you get it?" I glare at her. "What? I can't even ask about it?"

"No, you can't even ask about it. What the fuck, Misty? You want in this club or not?"

She huffs and crosses her arms like a child. "All right. Jeez." As she walked away, she whispered, "asshole."

I ought to flick her upside her head for that. If she were any other prospect, I would, or even worse. But a part of me admires her spunk. The kid really wasn't scared of anybody.

"Don't get that smart mouth popped," I say. She looks over her shoulder at me, stopping with her hand on the doorknob.

"Yes, sir. And by the way, Lillian says she'll see you tomorrow morning at camp."

That was good news. I was ahead of myself. I'd sent Misty to deliver the message before me and Flip headed off to get the scepter. I figure I need her expertise on the scepter. And besides, had we failed, it wouldn't have mattered if she agreed to see me or not.

"Thanks," I tell Misty.

She gives me an impudent smile and she says, "And also, your necklace is gone."

My hand goes to my chest automatically and I feel nothing but my shirt. I look down and see that she's right. It is gone. Shit. I must have lost it back at the museum. I stand up, debating portalling back there, then deciding against it. The place is probably crawling with Authority by now. I'd be a fool to go back right this second.

Still, I need that necklace. It's all I have left of Biz. I look at the clock and I decide to wait on it. Later, when the museum is closed, I'll go back and get it. Hopefully, nobody picked it up before then.

CHAPTER THREE

Eris

• • • • ● • ● • • •

"**W**OLF SHIFTERS," THE DETECTIVE says as he writes in his notebook. He hasn't looked up at me during this whole stupid interview. "You're sure about that?"

"I think I'd know a shifter if I saw one," I tell him defiantly. "I work in intelligence, remember?"

"Right, right."

I've been sitting in this utility closet next to the museum's security office for two hours now.

The makeshift 'interrogation' room would be laughable if not so damn uncomfortable. I fear the wooden folding chair has destroyed my back and the rickety card table is so disgustingly dirty I am not willing to rest even one finger on it.

I hate talking to Authority detectives. Even on a good day, they are supercilious and unbearably full of themselves. This detective is textbook when it comes to stupidity. He is treating me like I am a high society suit who got caught with her pants down. We're supposed to be colleagues, for cripes sake. I've told these guys everything and they still don't believe me. Ugh, it's ridiculous.

"So, these shifters, they just burst past the guards," the detective says, "push your date around and take the scepter. Is that it?"

I glare at him. Of course, that's not at all what I told him. "Do you have some kind of comprehension problem, detective?" I challenge him. He looks up at me for the first time since he sat down next to me on the bench.

"Excuse me?"

"You heard me. I didn't stutter."

I'm pissed now. How dare this asshole treat me like an idiot. Doesn't this jerk know I could have his balls in a sling before noon with a single phone call?

"Sorry, maybe that's your lack of intellect issue kicking in. I'd have that looked at if I were you."

His face is bright red and he looks like his head is about to explode.

Good. I hope he strokes out.

"That'll be all, officer."

I look over my shoulder to see my boss, Lynn, standing in the doorway. The detective's eyes jump from her to me and in a flash, I see him making the mental decision not to say whatever it was he was getting ready to say to me. I find myself wondering how long she's been listening as he makes the smart choice and leaves.

Lynn adds, "I'll see you in my office tomorrow morning, Detective Bryant."

All that redness drains out of his face. He knows he's fucked up. "Yes, ma'am."

Lynn sits down in his place, wrinkling her nose in disgust as she eyes the iffy table between us. She's wearing a stylish gray business suit and her blonde hair is up in a bun. She always looks like the height of style. My coworkers are scared to death of her, too. Her mind and her words are as sharp as that suit she's wearing.

"How are you doing, Eris?"

I feel a semblance of relief in having an ally. "I'm okay. Shaken up."

"I can understand that. I've been briefed. You weren't hurt, were you?"

I shook my head. "Is, uh...is Scott--?"

"I'm afraid Mr. Hibbert won't be committing any more date rapes anytime soon. The shifter made sure of that for what it's worth."

I nod. "I wish I could say that I am sorry. It's hard to feel bad about the death of a would-be rapist. So, you were briefed on everything?"

"Pieces of it," she says. "I'm hoping you can fill in the gaps. Why don't you start at the beginning? How do you know Scott Hibbert?"

I tell her everything from Ben setting up the date to Scott being late arriving to the shifter escaping through a portal. At that point, she stops me.

"A portal? Are you sure about that?"

"I know it sounds crazy, but he opened a portal. And the other guy spelled the door, locking it until after they left. Never seen anything like it."

She is quiet for such a long time I wonder if she believes me. "Do you remember the banishing of Christopher Opal?" she says finally. "A couple of years ago, I think it was."

I blink, puzzled, and caught off guard. That banishment polarized the world. I was fresh to the job when the wolf shifter was tried. His mage lover stood with him at his banishment, and when his people staged a rescue, he jumped into the portal with his lover, banishing—and probably killing—them both. The conflict and rumors about them being star-crossed lovers and all that split the human population up in a terrible divide for a while. The protests that followed were particularly bloody before they tapered off some six months later.

"Who could forget?" I say. "You think this robbery is related? I mean, Opal's banished. Probably dead. What's the connection?"

"Not sure. Opal could do magic. It's not been proven whether or not he could create portals. But we have enough credible reports of him using magic to be sure of some skill." She glances around us for a moment, watching for listening ears. Most of the guards and detectives are out of earshot of us. She still keeps her voice down with what she says next.

"We're fairly sure someone in his club could cast portal magic, though," she whispers. "According to several witnesses, club members seemed to appear out of thin air during the banishment. We figure if the leader knew magic, then surely others within the club did too."

"Oh, my Gosh. Why aren't any of them in custody?"

"Good question," she says with a hard laugh. "It's hard to catch someone who can wink out of existence whenever they want."

She looks pissed about that. I can't say I blame her.

"Do you think you can give a description of the shifter you encountered?"

"Sure. I'll do you one better. I'll look him up in the database."

Her brows knit together slightly, so I go on before she can speak. "I insist. I'd like to help you find the guy. He should not be on the street killing people."

She seems to give it a moment's thought, then she nods. "All right. But let the rest of us do the heavy lifting. Remember, you're the vic in this case."

She pats me on the shoulder, then gets up and motions for me to come. "I want a report on my desk by tomorrow. Let's keep this above board. I don't want this guy getting through the cracks."

"Of course."

We walk out of the museum together. It was after she drove away before I remembered the necklace. I haven't told anyone about it, and now it's burning a hole in the pocket of my dress.

This shifter intrigues me. He doesn't fit the profile. Everything I have ever studied about shifters clearly defines them as rage-filled creatures who tear humans to shreds at the drop of a hat. I think about how easily he snapped Scott's neck and how I could have been next. And then I think about how I wasn't next at all. He saved me from harm.

I wonder why none of the textbooks I've read mention how hot shifter men are? I don't know why I'm even thinking about this—he was really good-looking. He was tanned like he was naturally fair-skinned, but something in his face suggested a mixed heritage. At least to me. Maybe it was the dark of his eyes or the hollows of his cheeks and high cheekbones. Or his long wavy hair. It was in a ponytail, but a few tendrils escaped to frame his face as he fought with Scott. My mind was picturing it loose all over his head and my hands wanted to run through it.

Yeah, okay. So, he's hot. But he's still a shifter and there must be a reason why he fought to protect me. He didn't have to. Why should he care about some human getting attacked when his mission was obviously to steal the scepter?

There's no one in my office when I arrive, which is good. I don't want to be interrupted. I should have gone home, but my mind is buzzing about the shifter, and I want to know more. Questions. I have questions. He wore gang colors, a kutte meaning motorcycle gang. How are Opal's banishment, the scepter, and this shifter connected? The place to start is clearly the file from the Opal banishment and Opal's record...

***

Christopher Opal, aka Dire.

What a name. One look at his rap sheet demographics and it's clear why they called him Dire. The man was huge. I imagine he must have been a wolf the size of a small horse when he shifted. Truly a Dire wolf. It's funny how a guy that big, and an entire motorcycle club could stay hidden for so long.

The Maztecs. Not a single gang member is in custody. The ones we know the most about are dead and even still, we barely know anything about them. They're an elusive group if nothing else. As I flip through the mug shots it does not take long to find the man who rescued me.

Santiago Maguire, aka Mac. According to his most recent arrest, he was the club's vice president. Speculation has him as President after Opal's banishment. He's a shifter like Opal and is suspected of possessing the ability to control magic. According to the accounts of the Opal banishment, he headed up a failed rescue, but no arrests had been made.

This Maquire character got away scot-free. He got to live long enough to one day steal a national treasure and prevent the rape of one highly curious intelligence agent.

Why steal the scepter? He can't pawn it for cash, it's too well known. Not even breaking it up and melting down the metal would hide the source. The gold, the silver, and even the crystal gem are deeply imbued, at the cellular level, with magic that is recognizable to any mage. Countless mages have studied the staff and whatever active magic it contained died with Magnus Circadia.

This train of thought is a dead end. When he's in custody, perhaps I'll have the chance to ask him why.

I take the necklace out of the pocket of my dress and compare it to the picture on my screen. He was wearing this necklace in his mugshot. I rub my finger over the smooth amber of the pendant. It must have a high personal value. Clearly, it is special to him. Maybe if I did some research...find out where it came from, where it was made....

I stop myself before I start searching. It's like Lynn said, I'm the vic. I only need to lead them in the right direction. Point the Authority to his identity and let them go about finding him and the scepter. Easy enough.

Only if I do that, I'll probably never find out why he saved me. Shifters of his wanted level don't last long in prison before they're banished. And if he gets banished....

I can't get past wanting to know why he saved me. He had no reason to. Easy to see it was better for him NOT to step in. Scott was distracted and didn't even notice Maguire in the first place. He could have just done the deed and been gone before either of us was the wiser.

But he didn't. And because he stopped to save me, a man is dead and he just got identified by a GCI agent. When I file my report, they'll have him picked up before the day is out.

He's a criminal like any other. Saving me does not give him a walk. *Seriously, Eris? Are you thinking about not tagging him?* It comes to me then. He's an anomaly and I don't like it when events and people don't add up. I've never heard of or read about a single case of a shifter protecting any being other than their own.

Without warning the day's events catch up to me and I realize how late it is. I need sleep. Maybe in the morning, I'll have a better perspective. After all, why should I care about what a random shifter feels or thinks? I'm making more out of this than I should be.

***

The first thing I do when I get home from the office is take a shower. I feel dirty after the attack. Thank goodness Scott hadn't succeeded in his attempt to rape me. And, oh, my God, what kind of guy does Ben hang out with anyway? I really have to reevaluate my friend group.

I turn off the water in the shower and I reach for my towel. It's then I hear something outside my door. Or at least I think I hear something. The floors in my house are wooden and some of the boards creak when I walk on them. That was the sound....

It's my imagination. Or the house settling. This is not exactly a new place I live in. I wrap a towel around myself and start my nightly routine. As I'm putting moisturizer on my face, I hear the creak again and this time, I definitely hear movement.

I freeze, listening alertly. Someone is in my house. I glance around my bathroom for anything I can use as a weapon. There is nothing. It's a bathroom. I'll have to make a run for my bedroom, where I keep my taser.

I open the door slightly and peer into the dim light of my hallway. I don't see anything, but after a few moments, I hear furtive movement. Someone is definitely here. My heart pounds. I stand motionless as I evaluate my options. The first step, get out of this vulnerable position.

I take a deep breath and creep slowly out of the bathroom, moving toward my bedroom, staying close to the wall where the floor is less likely to creak. I slip inside and push the door closed, wishing I had a lock on it. Next step, Where did I put my phone? Shoot, it's in my purse in the living room.

Never mind that. Plan B. My taser. Whoever this is will find me and I need to defend myself. I quietly open my nightstand drawer and feel around for it. It's not there! Where is it? I never move it!

"Well, isn't this nice," I hear behind me say.

I jump and whirl around. Standing in the shadows is a man, bearded and wearing gloves. He smiles at me, showing teeth as sharp as daggers. I clutch the towel tighter around me and stumble backward, away from him. He steps forward and grabs my arm, yanking me so hard that my towel almost falls off.

"Where do you think you're going?" he breathes in my face. His breath smells like death. "We're just getting started."

CHAPTER FOUR

MAC

• • • ● • ● • ● • •

T HE NECKLACE ISN'T AT the museum. I've portalled in for a quick search. There's nothing here but an empty room buttoned up with crime scene tape at this hour of the night. My necklace is for certain not here. I rustle up a portal home and keep thinking this through. If the Authority had it, I'd be in custody by now. That necklace is as good as a fingerprint to ID me. The only other explanation is the girl. And this is a problem.

Soon as I'm back to the clubhouse, I go find Flip. He's sleeping in one of the rooms at the clubhouse since he and his girl split up. It suits him. This way, we can keep him busy while he mourns his relationship.

"Hey, Flip," I bark loudly at him. He starts awake, then looks over at me with cloudy eyes. "You're back on the clock. I need your technical expertise."

He sits up, looking over at his cell phone charging on the nightstand. "What time is it?" he groaned.

"Time for you to get your ass up."

He doesn't say anything else. He swings his legs over the side of the bed and takes a moment to rub the sleep out of his eyes. "Five minutes," I tell him and leave the room.

Flip's in the bar with me within four minutes. I don't waste any time. "I need you to find the girl from the museum."

He takes a beat before speaking. Then, "Okay. What for?"

"Not that it's any of your business, but she's got something of mine, and I want to get it back. Can you find out who she is?"

Flip frowns, but he takes a silent moment to think it through. "A random human whose name I don't even know? Sure thing." I glare at him and he clears his throat, remembering his place. "Sorry. Yeah, I can find her. No problem."

"Good. Get to it."

Flip's a lot of things. Irresponsible, a terrible judge of character when it comes to women, and a general fuck up. But he knows his way around the net and has a decent amount of arcane knowledge. There isn't anybody in the city he can't find, given enough time and effort.

This woman, it only takes him an hour to find. He worked on his handheld computer religiously until he came to me with a photo of her identification. Eris Loving, GCI agent.

"That's brilliant. Of all the women who I could have rescued," I said, more to myself than him. "Thanks Flip. Go back to bed. That's all I need for now."

She's got my necklace. Regardless of who she is, I need it back. Her address is on the card Flip handed to me. I pocket it and walk away from Flip.

Confused, I hear him say, "Where are you going?"

"I'll be back before dawn," is all I tell him.

Eris, of course, lives in the central hub where most, if not all, the humans in the city live, but according to her address, she doesn't live in the upper echelon which is interesting. She lives in the middle ring where a lot of the middle-class types live. I'm sure she makes enough money to live better and yet does not.

I file that information away in the back of my mind as I ride out there. What business is it of mine how she lives? I just need my necklace back.

**

The first thing I notice is how quiet the neighborhood is. My bike is loud and I'm sure I'm waking up people just riding down the block. I turn the bike off a block or so from her house and walk it up to park in her driveway.

There aren't any lights on, but it is late and she might be asleep. I ring the doorbell and wait. Nothing. I ring it again. After a few minutes, there's nothing again. I glance back at the driveway at the car sitting there. Clearly, someone's home.

I step back and look up, scanning the house. There could be a million different reasons why she wasn't answering. She might not want to answer the door to a biker this late at night. She could be out with somebody. Maybe catching a late-night drink with some friends. I mean, I don't know if I'd be in the mood for something like that if I'd been attacked a few hours ago, but who am I to judge?

I step off the porch when I hear a crash somewhere inside. The sound's followed by scuffling and suddenly, I'm on alert. I move into the shadows beside the steps and notice one of the windows is broken. Shit.

Kicking the door in is my first instinct. I decided against it, though. I've run the doorbell twice, so whoever's in there is watching and waiting for me to come charging in so they can jump me. I step further into the shadows and walk around to the back of the house, staying low so that I can't be seen through the windows.

I'm hoping there's a back door as opposed to a back window. Sure enough, there is. It's wooden, barely held together by plywood. I'm shocked that they didn't just go in this way. It would have been neater. I lean against the door, then give it a hard shove. It takes a few tries, but the door finally comes free with a loud crack.

The sound has no doubt given me away, but that's all right. Wherever they are, they're not in this kitchen. I step into the darkness and wait. Sure enough, a shadow comes rushing into the room. I jump behind him, wrapping my arm around his neck and squeezing. He struggles for a few seconds, but then he goes limp. I let him drop to the floor.

Somewhere in the back of my mind, I hear Pope in my head, admonishing me, even after all these years, when I'm doing something stupid. *Just leave. This isn't your problem. Yeah, sure. Not my problem. Just some assholes robbing a woman.*

There's no one in the living room or the den. There is one hallway leading, I assume, to the bedrooms. As I get close to the first door, about midway down the hall, I hear sounds of a struggle.

A female and a male voice, raised in conflict. Man, this can't be good. This poor woman can't catch a break. The voices become clear and I hear the woman yell, *Let me go! Stop!*

Nope. Not happening on my watch.

I turn the doorknob; grateful I don't have to kick it open. The tableau is classic; the man holding a woman down on the bed. What's not classic is Eris. She's fighting him with all she's got. Her hand is bound with his as they fight over the towel around her body. She's kicking her bare legs, flailing wildly, and just missing his balls with her knee kicks.

He's snarling, cursing, and breathing hard, using his weight to keep her down but she won't stay still and has scored deep scratches on his face and arms. I hope the blood I see is all his, but it's hard to be sure.

I charge across the room and tackle him away from her. We hit the nightstand and break apart, each of us leaping to our feet, ready to continue. The man narrows his eyes; it seems he recognizes me, but I do not know him.

I don't have another second to think about it because he pulls out a gun. I shift, diving at him again, this time full bore as a wolf. The gunshot explodes about the time I tackle him. The gun flies out of his hand, skidding across the room. He punches at me, trying to get out from under me, but it's no use. As a wolf, I outweigh him by at least fifty pounds. When it's all said and done, he goes still as he realizes I am holding him down with my mouth at his throat, poised to rip it out.

"No! Don't!" Eris is visible in my peripheral vision. She holds one hand out towards me and the other keeps her towel in place.

I pause. There are at least a million reasons for this man to die. I can think of only one reason to let him go. Not good enough. I can't let him go. Releasing a deep growl, I press my jaws over his windpipe. He grabs at my fur and his legs kick as his airway gets crushed.

"Stop! What are you doing? Stop it!"

I hold him there, waiting until his legs stop moving. When his arms fall to the floor, I release him, and then return to my human state.

She watches as my body changes and shifts. "You didn't have to kill him."

"He would have come back and finished the job."

Her eyes focus on my shoulder, and I realize it's bleeding. And smoking. This guy's bullet must have been silver. What is a burglar doing with silver bullets in his gun? I lean over the man's body and pat him down.

"Excuse me," she insists. "What do you think you're doing?"

"Ordinarily thieves don't walk around with silver bullets unless they're looking to rob shifters. I'm one hundred percent certain you, Princess, are NOT a shifter. I suppose this could be a case of mistaken identity; maybe he thought wolves live here."

In one of his jacket pockets, I find what I'm looking for. Walking over to where she stands by the bed, I hand her the license to read.

Her eyebrows lift in surprise. "What would a bounty hunter want with me?"

"Don't know. And it's hunters plural. I took out his partner in the kitchen." As I lean against a tall chest of drawers, I'm struck by how bizarre the situation is. This woman is a human. A high-level employee of the Cabal, even. What fool would put a bounty on her head?

"I'm calling the Authority." She turns to leave the room.

"I wouldn't do that if I were you," I say.

She stops and looks back at me. "Are you kidding me? This man broke into my house—"

"Bounty hunter. Not a man."

She closed her mouth with an audible smack, arms crossed tightly across her body. She was quiet for a long moment, shifting from one foot to another, her body echoing the indecision in her mind. "Maybe they are not really bounty hunters? Maybe the license is fake. Aren't bounty hunters mages?"

"Yup. This is the central hub and you're a human. If you're their target, they probably thought this would be an easy job."

The fear and confusion on her face changed and she stood up straight, clearly, I offended her. "What exactly is that supposed to mean? I'm not some weak girl, you know. I can take care of myself just fine."

"Of course you can, Princess."

"Excuse me? It just so happened they broke in while I was in the shower. If I'd been dressed...."

"Right, right. Look, put some clothes on. We need to get out of here. These guys might be bugged."

She scrunches her nose at me and I sigh. She is so out of her league here.

"They might have homing devices on them," I explain. "I don't care how tough you think you are, tackling bounty hunters isn't a game I care to play more than once a night."

She continues to stare at me. Indecision is easy to read on her face, and so is the moment she makes a decision. "I must be crazy. This is the second time today you've kept me from being seriously injured. All right. I'll go with you, at least until I figure out what is going on."

"I'll wait outside. Three minutes, no longer. Pack light. We'll be riding on my bike."

"Where are we going?"

"Somewhere safe," I tell her. "Oh, and I want my necklace back. Please. Bring it with you."

***

Outside, I check my watch. Of course, it's been longer than three minutes. How long does it take to fill a backpack?

I've been sitting on my bike, thinking. Humans are never on a bounty hunter's menu. This girl has a real problem. She must have gotten herself into some serious trouble to get a bounty placed on that pretty little head of hers.

I'm trying not to think about the towel. The memory of smooth brown skin and wet curls hanging down her back and over her slender shoulders keeps flashing in my head. She is a stunning beauty. Not like anyone I've ever seen before. She has a glow, her own light somehow. It's like there's a barely perceptible, golden aura around her.

After a good ten minutes, she comes out dressed in blue jeans and a dark blouse. The wet curls of her long hair are pulled back into a ponytail and she's got a backpack slung over one shoulder. She bops down the steps of her porch and then jogs over to me.

"Okay," she says. "Let's go."

"My necklace?" She reaches into her pocket and hands it to me.

"Get on."

She straddles the back of my bike as I put my necklace back on. When she wraps her arms around my waist it feels good. Natural.

"You are a good driver, right?" she asks, her voice shaky.

"I have to be," I say. "Hold on tight."

I back out of her driveway, then we tear off into the night with nothing but the wind in our faces and unseen danger at our backs.

CHAPTER FIVE

Eris

• • • • • • • • • •

I'D NEVER RIDDEN ON the back of a motorcycle before tonight. It was exhilarating. The wind in my hair and the way it cooled the skin on my bare arms. I leaned into his back, the smell of leather heavy in my nose as I held on as tight as I could. The fear of letting go and flying off into the night is as palpable as the excitement pumping through my veins. It's as close as I think I'll ever get to flying.

We rode for what felt like hours. I watched the night pass by at light speed, the scenery changing from that of my familiar and comfortable life to something else entirely. It was interesting to watch the world shift before my eyes. From clean, well-kept streets, to rocky and cracked cement roads, and then on to dirt roads. It was like we'd traveled through three different universes.

I'm certain we are heading for the city borders, but we're not going by any route I'm aware of. I don't see border gates or posts on the streets we're passing through. It's like we're traveling along some secret way. All I see is the world in darkness. A desert landscape against a clear night sky full of stars. I do my best not to look up at the sky for fear that I'll lose my grip on him and fall off, but what I see is beautiful. I've never seen the night sky look like this before. Shooting stars appear amongst a million glowing lights.

After a while, I see buildings and structures. Well, kind of. Most of them appear abandoned or blown up. Crumbling walls without roofs.

Half collapsed houses mixed in with debris from buildings completely flattened. This must be a part of the city that was destroyed during the war.

I've never seen this place in real life, only in photos. My research and lessons say places like this don't exist anymore; they were cleaned up after the war. Maybe this is not what I think. Maybe this is something that appeared after the war.

And yet, I'm not naive enough to think the history books I've studied are above being tainted. I see the evidence with my own eyes as we ride through this urban graveyard.

***

Maguire finally stops after an uncomfortable final ten minutes of bumpy navigation over ruts not meant for bikes to traverse. A high metal gate set amid an equally impressive riveted steel wall dwarfs us. It feels like it could eclipse the sunrise. He revs the motor then waves his hand.

"Smile for the camera," he says to me, looking over his shoulder as a low rumble, both audible and noticeable through ground vibration, signals the gate slowly sliding to one side, allowing us entry. "Welcome to El Castillo Maztec."

We stop in front of the patio area and he shuts off the engine after parking the bike.

As he helps me down, I look around. The gate behind us has closed on its own. I felt its rumbling as my feet first touched the ground, but silence reigns now. The patio stretches out in front of us and is obviously a gathering place with lawn furniture and grills dotting the open combination of mostly dirt yard and patched cement. A fire pit looks to be newly built, and someone has dotted the concrete benches surrounding the pit with colorful pillows. Obviously more than one person lives or at least frequents this clubhouse.

I wonder how long this building has been here? And how long it's been the Maztec clubhouse?

Did they find it and fix it up? They must have. The few windows are intact and well-maintained. It is obviously a re-purposed building, like many of those we passed on the way, but no longer in disrepair. I see pieces of cement where the paint is slightly chipped, but still showing colors from another time period, back when buildings all around the city were painted bright and lively colors.

"This is the Maztec home base. You'll be safe here," He steps aside and spreads his hand towards the entrance as if to say Ladies first.

I walk through the patio and up three steps to a deep, covered veranda dotted with rocking chairs. The whole building reminds me of pictures I've seen of an old restaurant chain. CrackerJack? CrackerBarrel? Something like that with a wide veranda filled with rocking chairs. Except for the wide front door which, I note, is also relatively new construction and appears to be reinforced with metal.

The first room we enter has the look of a dive bar. Although I'm betting it's not quite the same as the tame bars I occasionally hung out in during my college years. The place screams biker bar with beat up wood plank floors littered with sawdust, dartboards on the wall next to a barely legible Budweiser sign, and pool tables off to one side with a broken cue hanging off one, likely a casualty of a recent bar fight.

There's a heavy smell of stale beer and cigarette smoke hanging in the air. The tables filling the big room look like they've never been wiped down, all shiny with the sticky remnants of spilled beer. On the far side of the room, a huge bar spans the width, filled with a myriad of liquor bottles on shelves stacked to the ceiling.

"Through here," he says, leading me into a series of hallways to the left of the entrance. I'm grateful we stayed in the main hall. This looks like a quagmire of short halls created to split larger rooms. We pass by several doors and stop at the furthest one.

"You'll stay in here," he said. "I'll make sure to let the club know you're back here, so you don't have to worry about being disturbed."

The room smells a lot like the bar we just left. It's simply furnished and, appears to be clean. A single large bed fills most of the room. A plywood panel draped with the Maztek flag serves as a headboard. A dresser and a closet complete the decor. Nothing more, nothing less. I wonder if the doors we passed by are bedrooms like this one? Did all the club members sleep here? Did only some of them? My head is filled with unasked questions.

I nod. "Thank you...um...Sorry, I don't know what to call you."

"Mac," he says. "Just Mac is fine."

"Well, *Just Mac*, I'm Eris."

He smiles and says, "Yeah, I know."

I must have given him a surprised look because he followed with, "How else do you think I found your house, Princess?"

"Don't call me that," I say, narrowing my eyes. "You stalked me?"

He just chuckles like it's no big deal. "You had something of mine. Did you think I wouldn't come get it?"

"Actually, yes. You're not exactly a law-abiding citizen. I expected to see you behind bars, not in my bedroom."

He narrowed his eyes at me, and his smile faded. "Isn't that the thieving pot calling the kettle black?"

"Hey! I didn't steal that necklace. I found it where you left it, okay?"

"And what did you do with it when you found it?" He crossed his arms, irritation in his voice. "I'm sure you were questioned but you didn't give it up to the Authority. What dirty secrets did you find out about me, I wonder?"

I blink in surprise at him. "I'm not a fool, Ms. Loving," he says. "I know all about you and what you do for a living. When you watch us, we watch you right back."

I don't have a response. I'm chilled with anger. I'm also vaguely impressed with his intelligence. We look angrily at each other for a long moment. Then a spark flares between us, and for a split second, I see his eyes drift down to my lips just as I realize my own gaze is matching his.

The second passes. "Get some rest." He says, then steps out of the room and closes the door.

For a brief stunned moment, I stare at the door, then burst out laughing. There is clearly nothing funny about any part of this day. I walk over to the door and lock it behind him. Yeah, he said I'd be safe, but better safe than sorry at this point.

Suddenly, I'm exhausted and it's all I can do to slip out of my clothes and into bed where sleep comes fast. Until it doesn't. I woke up realizing I did not bring my medication with me.

"That's great. Damn."

This is more than an inconvenience. I have to take my medication every night or else I wake up with a horrible mind-splitting headache. And I missed taking it this morning, so it's going to be even more important I get it as soon as possible.

Nothing for it tonight. I'll have to get a new script filled and hope I don't feel like my brain is leaking out of my head in the meantime.

***

"Run! GO GO GO!"

I'm running as fast as my little legs will allow. There are others with me. Others like me. They're all so much taller than me and I can't keep up. Then he is holding me and running for me. I'm bouncing and holding on to his neck as tight as I can. They are coming. I don't know who 'they' is, but Papa says they will rip us apart if they catch us. We're different and that's bad. It's bad because we're the most different. Even those like us hate us.

"Here! Come this way!"

Her voice hits me like a gentle breath in my face. I turn towards it. She's standing halfway in and halfway out of a place. I know her. I've known her all my life.

"Hurry! Come on!"

Papa runs to her. I know she means safety. I know when I am with her, they won't get me. They won't—

Something is wrong. The others are fallen down. Papa is crying, I'm crushed between them when he holds her. She is crying, too.

She takes me from Papa and he kisses me, saying goodbye, before turning to the others who are so still, lying on the floor of the safe place.

She brings me to the fun place, where we cuddle and laugh, but this time there are only tears.

"Alura," she says to me and I know that word. It means me, so I pay attention. "Alura, you must stay here and be quiet. Be the quietest you have ever been. I pray they will take pity and this is the best we can do to protect you. You are too young to understand but know your papa and I love you forever." She lays me on the bouncy sleep place and covers me with a lot of blankets. I snuggle down and stay still. I like this hiding game.

The world is split with a loud boom and the air heats up all around me. The bed shakes and shakes.

I am tossed and get tangled in the blankets. Have THEY come? I wiggle out from under the blankets to find smoke and fire all around me. She is gone and so are the others.

I am afraid. Everything feels wrong. I look for the safe place, but it isn't there anymore. There's nothing but burning debris all around me. Nothing and no one. No one calling for me. No one looking to help me.

And then the man comes. He smells wrong. He brings the shadow and it falls on me and does not go away. I am alone and as he takes me away from the joy of the bouncy sleep place, I cry in fear and grief.

***

I open my eyes, my heart pounding like a drum. I'm breathing hard and shaking. I can't catch my breath.

It was just a dream. I'm...where am I?

It's then I realize my face is inches away from...from what? Is this drywall? I reach out to touch it and in doing so, I push my entire body back. As I turn my head, I see the overhead lamp above the bed right next to me. It's turned the wrong way around...why would that be...? What's happening? I look back at the drywall in front of me and I realize... Oh, God, am I ...am I floating?

The second I realize it, I fall back. I fall from the ceiling and onto the bed, landing hard against the springs before bouncing up and back onto the bed. I reach out and stop myself from rolling off the edge. I am breathing fast in a panic and force myself to take a deep breath and invoke calm. I look at the ceiling and the light fixture which was only moments ago right next to my head. I was floating? Was I really floating just now?

That can't be. I can't float. I lay with my arm over the edge of the bed, trying to process what just happened then sit up and look around the room.

It looks exactly as it had before I went to sleep. Still smells like beer. Still minimalist motorcycle club chic.

I'm losing my mind. That's it. I grab my phone from the charger on the nightstand and check the time. 3:03 AM. Clutching the phone as if it will anchor me to the real world, I lay back and force myself to breathe deeply in and out.

What a horrible, bad dream. It must have come from missing my meds. Bad dreams as a side effect. Who knew?

My heartbeat and breathing are back to normal, and I close my eyes, determined to think pleasant thoughts and fall back asleep. I'll ask Mac when he's awake to get my medication and everything will be fine. No more bad dreams.

After a while, my self-talk works and I drift back to sleep.

CHAPTER SIX

MAC

• • • ● • ● • ● • •

I STEP OUT OF the portal and am immediately blinded by the sunrise, already fully above the horizon. Odd that my magic again felt weak when I opened the portal, but I got it done. I must still be worn out from last night.

I turn and dismiss the portal and am now facing a waking camp. The resistance has moved a few times since I became president of the club. This is my favorite place they've found, and I hope they stay a long while. It's a lush environment with plenty of green grass and high-shade trees to hide the makeshift encampment. This time, their homes have an air of permanence, even though many are tented.

There's only one person I know who has enough knowledge about the arcane to help me figure out the deal with Magnus Circadia's scepter. I don't know how it works or even if everything people say Circadia used it for is genuine. For all I know, this scepter was nothing more than an ornament he carried around for clout; a glorified belt buckle.

Lillian is walking out to meet me. She's cut her dark hair into a pixie cut and is wearing a tank top and cargo pants today, looking very much the revolutionary that she is.

"Mac," she says as we hug in greeting. "So good of you to make time to visit."

"I miss our early morning chats, Lillian. It's harder to get away since Dire left."

"Yes, I've heard you are a busy man. Word around the campfire is you and your crew are into historical artifacts. Tell me that's a vicious rumor."

"I guess word travels fast," is all I can say.

She smiles grimly at me. "Risky business stealing a national treasure. Good to see you're still walking around. Hope it was worth it."

"I hope it was too. In fact, that's why I'm here. I hope we can talk history since you're the authority on all things arcane."

She sighs. "Mac…"

"No one I know knows more than you and I really need your help. I have to know everything there is to know about Magnus' scepter."

"Tell me you don't have it with you," she says.

"I thought you didn't like it when I lie to you."

The look she's giving me suggests a lot of things. Maybe pity or weariness mixed with wariness.

She's always had a soft spot for me and most of the time, if I have an ask, she does her best to comply. This, though. This is a big deal. It might be too much of an ask. We both know the kind of risk I'm taking being here with the scepter.

"If you were anyone else, I'd drive you out of here on a rail."

"I know. Look, I'm not asking for you to hold it or anything. I just need information about it."

She sighs again, then turns around and starts walking towards the center hut. "Come on," she says. "Let's not discuss this out in the open."

* * *

There's a folding table and folding chairs in a corner of the one-room hut. Her bed and personal belongings are neatly placed on the other side. A single comfy chair is in the far corner, in front of the stacked bookshelves filling the back wall. Lillian rarely stays in any single place for more than a few weeks or months at the most. Her life is one of a minimalist. The books are her only luxury.

She nods toward the table and I take a seat.

"Do I get to know why you took the damned thing in the first place?"

"Do you need to know why before you can tell me what you know about it?" I ask her, pulling the scepter out of my bag and setting it on the table.

She doesn't answer me. Her eyes are drawn to the silver shine of the scepter and its intricate carvings. She reaches out and picks it up, holding it one way and then the other.

"Wow," she whispers. "Thousands of shifters died because of this hunk of noxious gold and silver."

"They say it gave Magnus Circadia a massive amount of power. Enough to burn cities down."

"I'm aware of what they say," she says, setting it back down on the table. "You were in the war. What do you think? Do you recall a grand wizard standing atop a mountain with a flaming scepter laying waste to cities? We both know if that were true, there'd be a lot more destruction; there'd definitely be fewer of us around."

"So, what's the real story?"

"I can't tell this story without a cup of tea." She sighs, stands up, and walks to a stack of boxes serving as a kitchen counter. Pulling two cups from an open bin, she adds water from a bucket to an electric hotpot and turns it on.

"The beginning is before your time. Magnus Circadia's story is far more complicated than what is in the official public record. Not long after The Shattering that brought us here, he signed up as one of the thousands of mages who pledged themselves to the humans. At the start of the war, he rose quickly through the ranks."

"Who was he before he was a soldier?"

"A mage like any other," she says, "with a job and a family. I don't know how he became the most powerful mage ever. He found a way to draw on arcane powers unknown to the most skilled mages. By the time he was promoted to the rank of General, it's said he could manipulate time and space at will and move entire buildings with the force of his mind."

I raise my eyebrows in surprise. "Wow."

"Wow, indeed. But his magic was wild and not always under his control. He had issues with friendly fire. The scepter was intended to help him channel his magic, as a tool to help control power in more precise bursts."

As the water heated, she added tea leaves to a ceramic pot and brought the pot along with the cups to the table while continuing the story.

"Sugar?"

"Please."

"Magnus believed the humans of the Cabal were his allies, as most mages did and still do today. When the scepter was suggested to him, he eagerly agreed to be a part of the process. He did not suspect deception. I think he was a true believer and overwhelmed by the power he never expected to wield."

"The cabal was desperate to find a way to contain him entirely, not aid his control over the power. Humans can be stupid, as we well know, but the cabal leaders were not so stupid as to ignore Magnus. They feared the day he would turn his magic on them, and they did what they do best; they tried to control him, and when they could not, they destroyed him."

The hotpot boils and turns itself off with a click and Lillian pours the still bubbling water into the ceramic pot to brew. "When Magnus Circadia was presented with the scepter, he wasn't aware it was imbued with a special herb known to subdue magic temporarily. The herb has a subtle effect and is known to be cumulative over time, increasing the drain on a mage's power."

She brings the teapot and the sugar to the table as she talks. "What they hadn't anticipated was Magnus overcoming the power of the herb and laying waste to all who opposed the Cabal. Unbeknownst to him, he foiled their plan and eventually got stronger than he had been before the scepter's creation. Some theories suggest that the herb served as a catalyst to unlock his true power and enable his ultimate control over it."

She pours a cup of tea into one of the mugs and slides it to me and I add sugar and sip it slowly, digesting the information. "And he still had no idea that he was being betrayed."

"No. Not until it was too late. When the war was won, he was no longer of use to them. That's when he drops out of sight. The Cabal pushed the narrative he went to live in the outerlands, but that didn't make much sense."

"That's shitty."

"Tell me about it. That's the story of the scepter no one wants us to know. It's better for the Cabal if everyone believes the lies they feed us."

This is an interesting development, but I don't know yet what to do with the information. I sip my tea for a moment, and then ask, "What kind of herb did they use?"

"Don't know," she says. "I'm a lot of things, but an herbalist isn't one of them. I'd have to do research to find out. I do know it was a rare plant then. It's probably impossible to find now."

I picked up the scepter, turning it this way, letting it glint in the limited sunlight. "I'm surprised nobody's thought to use this thing since."

"That was his final joke on the Cabal," she said. "It became keyed to Magnus. No one's figured out how it works or how to use it. This lovely hunk of metal is nothing more than a giant paperweight now."

"Lucky us."

She nods in agreement, then smiles gently saying, "This has to do with your folks, doesn't it?"

Of course, she realizes my motivation. We've known each other since the war. She knows the mysterious circumstances under which my parents died. And she knows I've been looking to connect the pieces together since Biz died. "I don't know for sure. Maybe. My brother mentioned the scepter in his journal and I think there is a connection."

She nods again and sips her tea. "I guess that makes it worth all the trouble."

I look at the time on my cell and realize it's getting late. Eris has probably woken up by now. "I'd better head out," I grab the scepter and pack it in my bag again. "Could you do me a favor and find out what herb was used? And any other information about the scepter you can find?"

"Of course."

As I get up to leave, I remember the other question I had. "By the way, have you heard about any bounties on a human lately?"

Her eyebrows twitch and she cocks her head. "No, I don't think so. Why?"

"Somebody I know had a couple of bounties on them. Thought I'd ask if you heard something."

"You know a human? Since when?"

"Since last night," I chuckle. "If you hear anything, though—"

"You'll be the first person I call."

***

Stepping through the portal, no one's moving around in the clubhouse just yet. I go behind the bar and grab a drink from the fridge, then sit and think for a while. I only have pieces. I don't have the whole story yet. Magnus was betrayed by the Cabal. Fascinating, but I don't know what that has to do with my parents. One more piece to the puzzle. I just don't know where it fits. It's in my brother's journal and there has to be a connection.

CHAPTER SEVEN

Eris

• • • • ● • ● • • •

THIS TIME WHEN I awake, I'm solidly on and in the bed. No more dreams about wars and floating. I guess the medication is more powerful than I thought. Last night was an especially unique and stressful night. A girl doesn't get attacked twice in an evening every day, after all. Either way, I'd better find a way to get a refill today.

I shower and dress and as I walk out of the hallway, an MC member walks out of another room. He looks young and vaguely familiar. Thin with messy brown hair and a kutte that looks oversized for him. I think he's the one who was with Mac when he stole the scepter.

As soon as he sees me, he smiles and greets me. "Morning."

"Good morning," I say. "Do...do you work for Mac?"

His half smile turns to full. "Something like that. What can I do for you?"

"Well, Mac brought me here because...well, it's a long story. He wants me here for my safety. The thing is, I have to take medication for my migraines every day and I accidentally left the bottle back at my house."

"That's rough," he says.

"Yeah. I know Mac doesn't want me to go back to my house, but I can go into town and find a pharmacy—"

"That's a negative," he says, cutting me off. "If Mac wants you here to protect you, then you stay put. Somebody looking for you?"

"Something like that."

He sighs, his brows knitting together as he thinks about the situation. "Tell you what. I'm doing a supply run this afternoon. If you write down the medication, I'll see if I can get it for you."

"Would you? Oh, that would be wonderful. It's called, Levantus Doxate. It's for migraines."

He shrugged. "Never heard of it."

"I get it from my father's pharmacy, but I'm sure you can find it anywhere."

He chuckles. "You're dad's a pharmacist?"

"Yes. What's so funny?"

"Nah, nothing. It's just I've never met a pharmacist before. I didn't think they really existed."

I don't have anything to add. Who doesn't know about pharmacists? I feel like I'm in the twilight zone.

"Well, you haven't met him yet," I retort, "but like I said, I'm sure the medication is everywhere, so you won't have to go to my dad's pharmacy in the central hub or anything."

"I'll do my best to find it."

"Thank you." He gives me a pen and notepad from the pocket of his kutte, letting me write down the medication, and then he leaves. At least that's settled. I'll be glad to get my meds before I go to sleep tonight. I don't think I can handle another wild flying dream, not even a happy one.

I walk into the bar area just as a portal opens. It looks shaky as if it'll collapse any second. Mac walks through and the portal shuts. He looks back at the empty space as if a door was slammed on him. Well, that's confirmation of who's making the portals. It doesn't look like he's got very good control over it though.

He doesn't notice me at first, so I hang back in the shadow of the hallway and watch as he gets a bottle of orange juice from behind the bar and sits down to drink it. He is deep in thought and I'm in no hurry to interrupt him. I step back and lean against the wall to think.

This is really interesting. Shifters who can do magic. This is a revelation. It will turn the whole agency on its head when I get back. I don't think I ever conceived of a thing. It's like finding a new species of animal.

I step out and he nods at me. "You're awake."

"I am. Mind if I sit with you?"

He motioned his hand to the chair, encouraging me to sit across from him.

I probably shouldn't bring it up. I'm afraid to. But I have to know. I've never seen a shifter like him before. "I saw you come in. Through the portal."

He pauses briefly, then takes a drink from the bottle. "You caught me," he says. "Am I under arrest?"

"You're a funny guy. I didn't know shifters could do magic at all. Everybody says it's impossible. Not unlikely, totally impossible."

A knowing smile widens and then fades across his face. "Seems like we're both in the season for thinking things are one way and finding out something different altogether."

I tilt my head at him, but he doesn't explain any further. He seems contemplative this morning like thoughts are spinning around in his brain and he's trying to piece together a puzzle.

"Some of us can do magic," he says. "Mostly it's those of us who were born of a union between a mage and a shifter. Shifters imbued with magic is not as rare as the Cabal would have us believe."

"One of your parents was a mage?"

He nods. "My mother. I don't consider myself especially good at magic. I'm a much better Shifter."

"I see. All shifters who can do magic can create portals?"

"Absolutely not," he says. "That's a trick only reserved for a select few. I've only known one other shifter with the ability. He taught me. He tried to teach most of us in the club. I'm the only one who can reliably generate a portal. It's not easy magic and it takes a bit out of me when I use portals. If I can, I'll ride to a place before I portal over."

I lean into him, interested in knowing more about the magic I thought was exclusively used for banishing convicted criminals. "Must have been important to portal wherever you just were, then."

He doesn't answer that. He just drinks from his juice bottle.

"Can you portal anywhere you want?"

"Not exactly. I mean, I guess I could, but it works best if I've been in the place before."

He takes a long swig from the bottle, finishing it. "You hungry? I'm thinking about getting some breakfast. Want to come along?"

"Are we going to portal there?"

He snickers and stands up from the table. "I was hoping that we'd just take my bike, if that's okay with you." He holds out his hand to me like a gentleman. I have to admit, I like it a lot.

I take his hand and we leave the clubhouse. As I get on the back of his bike, I get that warm feeling again inside me the second I wrap my arms around him. There's something about him...something I can't deny. I hope I get to have this feeling longer with him.

CHAPTER EIGHT

MAC

· · · · ● · ● · · · ·

THERE'S A DINER I like not far from the border. We're riding and she's got her arms around my waist, clinging to me as we speed along. I can't help but wonder what it would be like to feel those hands against my bare chest or in my hair as she kisses me. Funny where the mind goes when the first sparks of attraction start.

I am drawn to Eris. When we sat at the table in the clubhouse, talking about shifters and magic, she leaned in, her dark eyes gleamed, meeting mine and showing true interest. She is intellectual, this one. Someone who studies and gets wrapped up in history books, I'll bet. I've never met anyone like her, and I like what I see.

At the diner, I help her off the bike and see her looking doubtfully at the building, taking in the cloudy windows and the half-lit sign above the door reading 'osene Pae' instead of 'Josene's Place.'

She wrinkles her nose skeptically and I snort a laugh. "Too rich for your blood?"

Her face melts into a good-natured smile. I take her hand and we walk inside.

Breakfast is one of the busiest times of the day for the diner, despite its location. We stand at the door, looking around for a free table for a minute.

Josene (I call her Josie), the owner, is walking to the cash register with a customer order in her hands. "Sit anywhere," she says without looking up. "Be with you in a second."

I spot a booth on the far side of the room. Eris slides in and looks like she's on the verge of a laugh.

"This place is...um...interesting," she says.

I shrug. "It's just a diner. Never been in one before?"

She shakes her head. "Sure, I've been in restaurants, but nothing to compare to this."

"Hello, dears." Josie walks up to the table with a pen and paper in her hand. "What'll you have?"

I just smile up at her. She is so busy, she hasn't looked over at me yet. "Still using that caveman tech, huh, Josie?"

She looks up sharply at me, then her face splits into a smile. Josie laughs and slaps my shoulder with the back of her hand. "Sandy Pants," she says. "How the fuck are you?"

I see Eris stifling a laugh. "I'm all right," I say to her, my face flushing. "Just treating a friend to breakfast."

She turned and looked at Eris, one elegantly arched eyebrow raising up skeptically. "Friend, huh? Well, any friend of Sandy Pants is a friend of mine. It's nice to meet you, dear."

"It's a pleasure."

"So," she says, turning back to me, "you run off with a motorcycle club and can't even call every once in a while?"

She says this every time, by the way. "I call you," is my normal response.

"Yeah, right," she retorts, just as she always does. "So, what's for breakfast this morning? No, wait. I'll surprise you. Something special for you and your guest."

She turned and left without another word and Eris busted out laughing as soon as she was gone. "Wow. 'Sandy Pants'?"

"Only she gets to call me that," I say. "So, don't get any ideas. That name dies right here."

"No problem," she says, unsuccessful in stifling her laugh. "You seem close."

I pause, wondering how much to tell her. We have only just met. I suppose basic information wouldn't hurt much. "My parents were killed during the war," I tell her. "She took me and my brother in for a couple of years after that."

"You were war orphans," she says and sees my grimace. "What?"

"I don't like it put that way. My parents weren't warriors. They weren't involved in the action. They were just people living their lives. One morning, my brother and I got up for school and found them gone. Their beds are empty, and their clothes and car keys are still in their places. They disappeared into thin air."

She looks at me with large mournful eyes. "That must have been terrifying."

I nod, the memory of being the older brother filled with worry and trying not to telegraph it to Biz. He was only fourteen to my sixteen at the time and he was smaller and frailer than me. I had to protect him.

"The first night we didn't know what to do or who to call. We thought they would come home. Thought for certain by the next morning, they'd be back with a crazy story to tell us. Then one night turned to two and that turned to seven and by the end of the week, we were looking for food in garbage cans. The big scare was only beginning."

"Jesus, I...that sounds terrible. I'm sorry you had to go through that."

I look at the pity on her face and I don't like it. I don't like that she's looking at me like I'm a charity case. "We did OK. Eventually, Josene took us in, and, uh, the rest is history." It's the best way I can end this discussion. We didn't come here to listen to my sob story of a life.

"Tell me about your family," I say, changing the subject.

She shrugs, looking down at her hands with embarrassment. "It's...it's nowhere as interesting. I mean, I'm just a human from a human family who, up until last night, lived in the central hub."

"Can't possibly be that boring. Any brothers or sisters?"

"Nope. Just me."

"Both parents alive?"

"Yeah. Mom's a homemaker with a part-time job as a teacher's assistant, and my dad's a pharmacist."

I laugh and she joins me, shaking her head. "Oh, wow," I say, "You're serious?"

"What is with you MC guys?" she asks with a laugh. "You know, I ran into one of your friends when I came out of my room this morning. When I told him, he laughed, too."

"Why would you tell one of my people about your dad?"

"I need my migraine medication and he said he would pick it up for me. That's not important. What I'm saying is that he thought it was weird that I was the daughter of a pharmacist. Do criminals not need pharmacies?"

"No, we don't," I say in all honestly, but also with a laugh. "There's also no caviar or thousand-count sheets."

"Oh, stop that. This is basic health care we're talking about, not a million dollar-a-night hotel."

Josie returns with two plates of pancakes with hash browns. The pancakes are stacked high and fluffy and covered in syrup and butter. "There you are. One special breakfast hot and ready."

"This looks amazing," Eris says with a smile. "I can't believe how good this looks."

"It does look pretty great. Thanks, Josie."

She looks at me with a big motherly smile and says, "It's on me, provided you call me every now and then."

"I always do," I say. She gives me a pat on my shoulder, then goes back to the other customers.

We eat and talk and for this time, nothing else in the world matters. Those things that brought us together, bounty hunters and the Authority looking for me, that's somewhere else right now. Now it's just the two of us talking and I'm completely enamored with her. I thought I had her number when we met and now, I realize she's nothing like I was expecting.

I don't know what's happening here, but for the first time in a long time, I'm actually connecting with someone and it's the most unlikely person I could have met.

***

"Those pancakes were amazing," says Eris as she wipes spots of syrup from her lips. "I don't think I've ever had anything like them."

"You ought to slum it more often," I say with a wink. "I mean, I don't know but I've been told, that the food's better down here."

"I don't know about all that, but the pancakes were definitely phenomenal."

We share a smile together, and then I say, "Let's get out of here."

We leave the diner, waving goodbye to Josene on the way out. In the parking lot, I suddenly don't feel like I'm in a great rush to get back. "What do you say to walking these pancakes off?"

She raises an eyebrow at me. "If you think I'm going to walk all the way back—"

"No, no. Come on." I take her by the hand and lead her around the diner and onto a path into a short patch of woods behind the diner. I had the initial thought that she might pull away or maybe fight me on this somehow, but she doesn't. She lets me lead her. I guess I've earned some modicum of trust.

There is a small patch of wood behind the diner that opens into a field of sunflowers. I've never been sure how this place exists in the middle of a ruined city. It's still here, even after all these years, still thriving and growing. When we break through the wood, we stand at the edge of a field that seems to stretch all the way to the blue skyline beyond.

"Oh," Eris whispers. "What...what in the world?"

"What's the matter?" I give her a nudge. "They don't have sunflowers in the central hub?"

She walks up to one of them. These in front of us are young. Barely taller than I am. She touches one of the petals as it leans down over her. "No."

Well. That's a surprise. I couldn't have heard her right. "Did you say no?"

She nodded. "I mean, I've seen photos, you know. Things about how the city used to look before the war...but I've never actually seen anything like this before. They're so...big. Why are they so big?"

"They're sunflowers. They're supposed to be big." I walk up next to her, running my hand over the flower's head. "They get bigger than this, too. When I was a kid, there were sunflowers in this field the size of grown men."

She looked around us for a long moment, trying to process what I'd just said to her. "Are there more fields like this around here?"

"Not that I know of. Most precious places like this didn't survive the war."

Eris' smile drops and she looks at me, brows knitted together in confusion. "What do you mean, 'precious places like this'?"

I gesture towards the field. "Fields of flowers, roses, the colors of nature, green and yellow flora and fauna. They are gone from this place."

She looks at me for a long time, then she asks, "Why don't you like the term war orphans?"

I'm taken off guard by the out-of-the-blue question, but I answer it. "I refuse to be a victim. I saw your pity when I told you about my parents being killed during the war. I am no one to be pitied."

She nods slowly, accepting what sounds to me like a perfectly reasonable response. Then to my surprise, I feel her hand slide into mine, interlocking with my fingers. She moves close to me, then brings her lips up to mine. I'm taken aback by this kiss, warm and sweet against my lips.

I pull back and whisper, "Why did you do that?"

"Because I wanted to," she replies, then kisses me again. I wrap my arms around her waist and embrace her fully, the kiss becoming more passionate. She takes my lips between hers the gentle pressing of her teeth against my skin. It's been a while since I've had sex with anyone, but it feels to me like this is where we might be heading.

Do I want sex with her? I've been taught my whole life that human women were always bad news. Always looking to trap one of us with the promise of exotic sex. I've been playing with fire up until now with this whole relationship. I suppose there's no reason why I shouldn't go with this.

I feel her hands move down my chest, going under my shirt and running over my abs, feeling their way up to my chest. I feel her gentle nails drag across my skin and the sweet and slight sting sends chills up my spine. I suck in air between my teeth and I whisper, "Careful. Don't start anything you don't want to finish."

She smiles against my mouth slightly, then she moves down to my neck with gentle kisses. In the next instant, she's on her knees before me, unbuckling my belt. I'm still stunned by her forward actions. I watch as she unzips my jeans and pulls out my manhood. Her hand encircles it moving up and down in slow, smooth motions. She teases me with her tongue, rolling it around the head. I'm caught in the middle between enjoying this sensation and being hungry for more. Her lips wrap around my cock, finally. She takes my length down her throat, sucking in slow strides.

If you'd told me this morning would end up with a blow job in a sunflower field, I'd have laughed you out of the room. But here I am with her sucking me off, moans vibrating around my shaft. I move my hips, daring to thrust deeper down her throat. She takes me with skill, her lips hitting the base repeatedly.

I could blow right now. If she keeps this up, I could. But...I don't want that experience with her. The fear that I'll come and she'll get back up and walk away from me as if she'd just paid me back for the deed of protecting her comes over me. I don't want her like that...

I take hold of her head and slow her down. She looks up at me questioningly as I say, "Get up."

She releases me and stands up. I take her in my arms and kiss her gently. Then I take off my kutte, tossing it down on the ground. "I want you," I growl. She's taking off her shirt and I'm taking off mine. I kiss her neck, the hollow of her collarbone. Her bra strap falls down her shoulders as I run my tongue between her full breasts.

We move down to the ground together and she pushes away from me just long enough to get out of her pants. Once the pants are off, she straddles me, allowing me to enter her. I'm surprised at how tight she is and it makes me moan as she utters a shaky gasp. Her hands are on my chest as her hips move, rocking back and forth on top of me.

I'm in heaven. Among the sunflowers and the blue sky above me, I could die and it would all be fine. My hands move over the soft skin of her belly and she smiles at me. "Say it again," she moans breathlessly. "Tell me you want me."

I feel my fangs start to show themselves. Seeing her brown skin in the sunlight, her curls falling into her face...she seems to glow in her own light. It's like I'm being fucked by a goddess. "I want you," I moan. "Fuck...I want you so bad."

She bites her lip, squeezing herself around me. She leans back and unhooks her bra. As it falls over her arms, I slide my hands up to her breasts, my thumbs rubbing over her rock-hard nipples.

Her eyes roll back and she speeds up her rhythm. I grab hold of her hips and thrust, diving deeper inside her. The pitch of her soft moans climbs, reaching the sky as her body shivers. God, watching her right now...looking at her glorious body...my claws come out and pierce her skin leaving thin red lines along her hips.

"Oh, yeah..." she cries out, "oh...Mac...yes!"

She explodes at the same time as I do. I feel my body jerk and the animal in me comes out in a howl that starts in my chest and spirals up into the heavens.

And when it subsides, our eyes meet. She runs her hands over my sweaty chest. Then she smiles. "Your fangs are showing," she says.

She moves her hips slowly against me, taunting me...tempting me for another round. I oblige. I could spend eternity inside her.

CHAPTER NINE

Eris

• • • • ● • ● • ● • • •

W E'RE LYING IN THE field of sunflowers. My head is against Mac's chest, listening to his heart. I wanted this. I have no explanation for why I kissed him except that I wanted to. I'm attracted to this man. Terribly attracted. I've been drawn to him almost since the first moment I saw him. And now...now it's just us under the sunlight. Everything else can wait. I will wonder later why I would do something so out of character and not regret it for a second.

As if he's reading my mind, he says, "We should get back to the clubhouse."

I sigh. "It's so beautiful here."

"There are other beautiful places."

"Any place like this?"

He shrugs. "Maybe. I know of at least one place just as beautiful as this. Maybe even more so."

I lift my head and look at him. "You do? Somewhere outside the city?"

He's looking into my eyes, reading me. Trying to see if I'm being for real, maybe. "There are a lot of places that nobody knows about," he says. "Places that would be a million times better to hide than in this city."

"Why don't you live there, then?"

"Still got work to do," he says. "Wars to fight...all that."

That raises a lot of questions. What wars? What work? What is he talking about that I'm not connecting? I start to ask when his phone rings. He squeezes my shoulder and kisses me on top of my head.

"Speaking of work," he says as he sits up and reaches for his pants. He pulls his phone out and answers it. "Yeah?"

I lay there for a moment, wondering how I could convince him to go just one more round. Whatever is going on, surely it can wait...

I see his back stiffen as he goes quiet. I get the innate sense that something is very wrong. A strange swirl of terror swirls within me and I sit up with him. He glances over at me briefly.

"Are we whole?" I hear him ask. I don't know what that means, but whatever it is, he receives the right answer because I can feel him relaxing. "All right. We're heading back now."

He hangs up the phone, then stands and says, "Come on, get dressed. We have to go."

I start grabbing my clothes. "What's going on?"

"Our supply run got hit. Bounty hunters."

My stomach drops. The same ones who were after me. As I put on my clothes, I can't help but wonder if the attack is my fault.

He looks at my face and pauses. "This isn't about you." His voice is gentle but certain.

"How can you be so sure?"

"Hunters are always looking for us," he says. "This is just another Wednesday for us, Princess."

It takes only a few minutes to dress and be on the bike pealing out of the diner's dirt parking lot. This time, riding on the back feels less exhilarating and more terrifying than anything else. I don't know what's in store for me when we get back to the clubhouse and I can't help wondering if he's wrong. Bounty Hunters might be coming for the MC, but then why do I feel like this is my fault somehow.

Then it hits me. The supply run. The one MC member I ran into said something about making a supply run that afternoon. That had to be it.

We get back to the clubhouse in record time. When I get off the bike, I turn to Mac and ask him, "Where were they when they got hit?"

He pauses, thinking, then, "Not sure yet. Why?"

I shift my foot from one to the other. Goddammit. He could get pissed at me if I tell him.

"Spit it out, Princess."

She takes a deep breath. "My medication," I say to him. "Remember, I told you I asked one of your guys to get my meds and—"

"You seem pretty determined to make this about you, Eris."

I feel my face flush as a rush of anger hits me. "Excuse me, but I'm only trying to help."

"You can help by keeping your head down and keeping quiet while I handle this."

He walks away from me. I follow, steam coming out of my ears.

The bar is the reverse of what it was a few hours ago. Almost every table has someone sitting in it and almost everyone looks beat up and bruised. A few of them have one of the others taking care of their wounds and bruises, and for the most part, the bar looks like it's being used as a triage from a war.

The biker I met that morning walks in. He's carrying a big box of ice packs. He walks around the room, tossing them to members who need them.

"Flip."

The biker looks up at Mac, his face splitting into a smile. "You're back," he says, setting the box aside and coming over to us. "Good. We were worried about you being out there alone."

"What happened?"

"Just a regular run. Everything was smooth until on our way back. Out of nowhere, a bunch of hunters on bikes jumped us. Hunters on bikes! Can you believe that? Assholes are upping their game."

"Were you able to get anything through?"

Flip shakes his head. "We had to leave it all. It was either that or..." He trails off, but we both know what he means.

"So," I speak up, "you never got to the pharmacy for my meds?"

"Actually, we did," Flip says. "Sorry. The guy said they were out."

"Listen," Mac says, "Get everyone together for Church, all right."

"Sure thing, Mac." As Mac walked away to tend to one of the other members, I stopped Flip.

"You said that guy said they were out," I say. "Where did you go?"

"Closest one to the border. No offense or nothing, but we weren't going to risk going into the central hub."

I nod. "Right, of course." I let him go. I didn't think they'd actually take a risk like that, but I had to ask.

A young member walks up to me. She's wearing a kutte like everyone else, but hers has no patches on them. She's thin with long, shoulder-length dark hair. "Mac says you should get to your room. If you need anything, I'm supposed to take care of it for you."

I can feel a dull headache starting up behind my eyes. Uh-oh. I guess it was too much to hope for that I'd be okay without my meds. "Yeah, sure," I say to her. "The one thing I need was supposed to be in that supply run."

She shrugs. "We'll try again," she says, "Soon as they get themselves square. My name is Misty, by the way."

She puts out her hand for me to shake and I do. "Eris."

"Oh, we all know who you are. You kind of stand out like a sore thumb."

"I guess I do at that."

***

I've been in this room for hours and my head feels like it's going to explode. Shit. I need my meds.

I lay on the bed looking up at the ceiling and the memory of my dream of floating comes back to me. I kind of wish I could float right now. Right out of my body and away from this pain.

I hear a knock at the door. "Eris. It's me. Can I come in?"

I'm still pissed at Mac for dismissing me earlier. I've got a good mind to tell him to fuck off. My manners know better, though, so instead, I say, "Yeah."

The door opens and he comes in. His long hair is hanging loose and he looks tired. He's got dark circles around his eyes and his shoulders are slumped forward. I sit up, trying to ignore the throbbing behind my eyes. He pauses, cocking his head as he looks at me.

"You okay?"

"Not really," I say. "Migraine."

"Ah. Right. Your meds."

"My meds."

He sighs and sits down on the bed next to me. "I'm sorry about all this. You shouldn't have to go without your medication."

He rubs my shoulder to comfort me and I lean into him, resting my head on him. "I've never missed a day," I say. "I guess I forgot how annoyingly disabling this can be."

He doesn't say anything for a moment, so I say, "How was...what did you call it? Church? God, I don't even know what that means."

"It's a way of saying we need to meet for important shit," he said. "Church went okay. Learned that the bounty hunters spotted the crew at some point and decided to follow until they got close to the border. Thankfully, they were stupid enough to jump the gun instead of following through. We might've led them straight back here."

"Do we know why they attacked you?"

He takes in a deep breath. "We're shifters," he says. "That's reason enough. But if I had to guess based on how many of them and how organized I'm told they were, I'd say it's because of the scepter. I'm sure we all have targets on our backs because of that heist."

I don't really say anything to that. I don't know why Mac stole the scepter in the first place and I don't think I want to know. I'm in enough trouble all on my own as it is.

"Sorry for barking at you earlier," he says out of the blue. "I had my work hat on and...around here, nobody questions me."

"That's no excuse," I say wearily. "Aren't I your girl or something now? You have to treat me differently."

He chuckles. It's just a few quick breaths against the back of my neck. "You presume a lot, Princess."

"I told you to stop calling me that," I say.

"Sorry." He takes a deep breath as we sit in silence, then, "Let me make it up to you. Why don't we portal to your apartment and get your meds?"

I look up at him and frown. "Didn't you say that doing portals is exhausting?"

"You exaggerate. I said it's tough, but I can still do it. You look like you're suffering quite a bit."

I nod. Truthfully, the thudding is starting to subside, but still, it's nice of him to offer. "The bounty hunters will probably be at my place. I don't really know how wise that is."

"Are your meds in a part of your apartment that I've been in?"

"My bedroom. What difference does that make?"

"If I've been in the room before, it makes the process a lot easier."

I'm still giving him a skeptical look. What if we portal in and some hunter is rooting through my personal things?

"It'll be fine," he says, putting a reassuring hand on my knee. "We'll zip in, you'll grab your meds and we'll zip out. We won't be there but a few minutes."

"What if there's somebody there?"

"I'll handle them."

I bite my lip, thinking about the scar he's got on his shoulder from the last time he tangled with one of them. The right bullet could kill him and then what?

He squeezed my leg. "It'll be fine. Promise."

I laugh. "You can't promise that."

"Just did. Come on. You can't go without your meds, right?"

He was right about that. I don't think I can handle this pain all the time. I sigh finally and say, "All right. But in and out. No dallying."

"Gotcha."

CHAPTER TEN

MAC

• • • • • • • • • •

LIKE I TOLD ERIS, this shouldn't take but a minute.

We portal in, we find her meds, we're out. The only problem I can think of encountering is a bounty hunter in her bedroom and I don't see that as being likely unless they happen to be looking for something.

Which they might be, I guess. I still don't know why they want her.

I take her by the hand, and we stand up. "You ready?"

She nods. "Okay," she says, "Let's go."

I summon my power and wave one hand. The wave isn't really necessary, but when there are people about, they expect to see something, so it's a habit I've developed. A portal opens in the room, and we can see the colors of Eris' bedroom behind the shimmer.

She pauses, squinting as if trying to look before she leaps.

"Come on," I say, my hand is still holding hers as I lead her through the portal.

We're in her room a second later and she pauses, taking a deep and shaky breath. I put my finger to my lips to shush her, then I move to her bedroom window to look out into her backyard. There are a couple of bounty hunters walking around with their hands on the guns at their hips. Patrolling. As expected.

"Is it safe?" she whispers.

I shake my head. "Hurry up and get your meds so we can go."

She walks over to the nightstand and opens it, grabbing a small glass jar from the contents. She turns the lid to open it, but I stop her. "Let's go. If they're outside, they're probably around the house too."

"Right," she says, closing the jar and joining me before the shimmering portal just as it flashes out of existence. Shocked, I summon my power...but nothing happens. No warm surge in my gut or spark of electricity in the air. I don't feel anything.

Eris looks over at me. "What's wrong?"

"I don't know," I close my and push deep into my psyche to sense the magic, but it's eerily quiet. The arcane is simply gone from in and around me. Since I was a teen, power has been a viable piece of my world. It's a living force. The air is empty. It feels like I'm chewing a piece of cardboard when I expect a spicy sausage. What the hell?

When does it ever fail? Bad goes to worse. Before I can even think about what my total loss of magic could mean, the door opens. A man wearing a dark jacket and blue jeans with a silver gun on his hip walks in. The second he sees us he freezes, mentally processing our faces, and clearly as surprised to see us as we are him.

Shit. I jump for him as he reaches for his gun. I manage to grab him by the wrist, knocking the gun out of his hand and across the room. He pushes me off and throws out his hand, obviously intending to throw a burst of magic at me...but nothing happens. He looks down at his hands for a moment in shock.

Yeah, I know where you're comin' from, buddy, but I'm not waiting for you to recover. I jump at him, knocking him back against a wall, and call on my wolf. The push to shift hurts like a sonofabitch and I can barely sense the wolf. We push together and my claws and fangs form. Just in time, I grab him by the throat, claws digging into his skin.

He struggles, gagging and grabbing at my hand. A second later, he brings his leg up and kicks me in the shin, sending me to the floor. Once freed, he kicks me again and I fly back, accidentally bumping into Eris and landing on the floor.

She stumbles and I hear glass break and realize her medicine jar has shattered as tiny purple pills mixed in with the glass spread across the floor.

The hunter has his boot raised, intending to stomp me.

I roll out of the way as his steel-reinforced booted heel smashed into the floor behind my head.

Instantly, I roll right back, knocking into his leg and sending him sideways, falling into the opposite wall with a loud thud.

Voices yell out from behind the bedroom door; the others are coming, and I can't get us out of here. Shit, shit, shit! I get to my feet as the first guy breaks through the door and comes at me. We grapple for a second, then two more appear in the open doorway.

I push the first guy into them, but they dodge out of the way, each side stepping in opposite directions. The first guy tumbles out of the room, knocking up short against the opposite wall and jumps back up coming back into the room. The three of them draw guns and stand side by side grinning at us.

The sound of three guns cocking was surprisingly loud in the room.

I'm fucked now. For sure, they're loaded with silver.

"No!"

What happens next is so fast that I can barely comprehend it.

No sooner does Eris shout, than a blast of fiery magic shoots past me and into the two hunters, sending them straight through the wall and obliterating what remained of the door. Fire engulfs the wall and pieces of it rain down. Burning drywall is shattered into a million pieces and raining down on the bodies of all three fallen hunters crumpled against the door across the hall.

I stare at the wreckage for a moment, astounded, then turn to Eris who is frozen in place, arms outstretched. Her hands are engulfed in blue smoke. Her mouth is agape and her eyes are wide open.

What the hell was that?

"Eris."

She doesn't move. Her body has begun to shake uncontrollably, and I see raw terror in her tear-filled eyes.

I touch her shoulder gently and she jumps back, blinking fast.

"Hey," I say, taking her by the shoulders. "Eris. Look at me."

Her eyes turn to me and for a second, I don't think she sees anything. Then slowly, I see her focus on my face. Her bottom lip quivers and in a squeaky voice, she says, "M-mac..?"

"It's okay," I say, and I press gently to bring her arms down.

She stiffens at first, then goes with it and lowers her arms.

"Come on. Let's get out of here." I take her wrist, wary about touching either hand, and we leave the bedroom, stepping over the unconscious men in the hallway. Or dead. That was some blast, after all.

We move through the living room quickly. I'm keeping a watch for any other bounty hunters. Fortunately, I see none...at least not yet.

I don't know how we're getting back since my magic is on the fritz but running seems like the way to go. We run along the sidewalk, keeping to the shadows of the trees hanging over the street in spots. I think I hear sirens in the distance. We have to get off this street.

It's about midway down the next block when I feel the air change around me. Could my magic be back? I stop and try summoning my energy again. This time I feel the magic respond, and I reach out to create a portal home.

Eris stares blankly at the portal. She is still stunned and shaky. "It's okay," I whisper. "We're almost out of this."

I wrap an arm around her shoulders and move her side-by-side to jump through the portal. A second later, we're back in the bedroom at the clubhouse. The portal closes and for a moment, we just stand in silence.

Eris takes a few steps back. She's holding her hands together tightly in front of her and staring off into nothing. She keeps stepping back until she reaches the bed, then she flops down.

I don't know if she can hear me. I don't know if she can answer. But I have to ask. "What the hell was that?"

She just looks up at me and I see water in her eyes again. I don't think she knows any more than I do.

CHAPTER ELEVEN

Eris

• • • • • • • • • •

I DON'T KNOW HOW long I've been sitting here. What happened? How? I don't think I believe it. I mean, what is happening to me?

When I didn't respond to Mac, he left, saying he'd be back in a second. At least, that's what I think he said. I'm out of my head at the moment. Or maybe in my head. Everything sounds like it's coming from a tin can and I feel like I'm floating out of my own body right now except that I can see my legs hanging over the bed and my feet touching the floor.

My hands. I can't look at my hands.

I keep seeing it happen in slow motion in my mind. Mac fighting the first hunter. Then the other hunters ran into the room and pulled their guns. They were going to kill us both. I knew that with every fabric of my bones. Mac knew it, too. I heard the words in my mind. They are going to kill us both.

When I raised my hands, I didn't think about it. It was defensive instinct. I felt hot. Really hot and flushed. An ache formed deep in my core and spread through my body. There was a flash of light and the ache, the heat left me.

I saw the light split. I saw it hit each of them in the chest. I saw it hit so hard their bodies lifted off the floor and flew backward into the hall like ragdolls. I saw them hit the wall so hard that cracks appeared in the drywall. I saw the light spreading out and breaking the whole wall between and around them. I saw each hit the wall across the hall and crumple like ragdolls.

Everything happened before my eyes in agonizing slow motion.

There's a low hum of the air around me. Has been ever since it happened. I don't know what it means, but the air is different. I am different.

I look down at my hands. No blue smoke. No heat. No tingling sensation. Two normal hands. It's like the flying dreams. I want it to be a dream. Can I make myself believe it was a dream?

Mac. He saw it. Saw them fly back. Saw their bodies impact the wall and break. He witnessed my power firsthand.

My... Power? How? I don't understand. I'm human. I'm a human being. How can I have arcane powers?

"Eris?" Mac is standing before me, holding two bottles of beer. He hands me one and sits next to me.

I look at the bottle, the cool glass feeling good in my hands, yet...this isn't exactly what I thought he would bring me. "I was expecting a glass of water."

"Yeah," he says. "I was going to bring one back, but then I figured you probably would do better with a drink."

That's fair. I take a swing from the bottle and wipe my mouth with the back of my hand. We sit and drink in silence for a few minutes before Mac asks, "Want to talk about it?"

Just him saying that starts my eyes burning. I feel like I might break down sobbing, so I take another swig, swallowing the urge back down. "I don't know how to talk about this. How do I talk about this, Mac?"

He thinks for a moment, silently dangling the beer bottle between his knees. "I don't know," he says softly. "This is uncharted territory for both of us."

"There must be an explanation," I say to him. "There has to be."

"Evolution, maybe?" He shrugs, clearly unsure of his answer.

I glare at him.

"What? Humans evolve. Isn't that science? Maybe you're the first of a new type of human. One who does magic?"

I think about that. Nice idea. It would have been great when I was in middle school. There were a few bullies who could have benefited from a fire blast every once in a while. I think every kid wants to be a superhero in that way, right? Fantasy. Sketches in a notebook. Angsty teenage words in a diary. But I've studied mages and mage magic in my job and I know magic doesn't manifest suddenly in adults and never in humans. There's never been a case of either.

I shake my head and say to Mac, "No. Magic manifests in mages when they reach puberty. I'm about ten to thirteen years past that."

"Right. Of course, you would know that." He takes a swig from his bottle

I ignore the comment. "It's more likely this is some kind of fluke," I say instead. "Or maybe a side effect of my medication or—"

"You've been off your meds all day," he interrupts. "How can there be side effects to something you're not even taking? You know, it could be the answer is simpler. Maybe you're part mage."

I roll my eyes. "I'm not part mage. Both my parents are human. In fact, there are no mages in my family line. I'm not even a quarter mage."

"You sound awfully sure about that. One of your family members could have been a mage in hiding. People find ways around the system all the time."

I scowl at him. That's a ridiculous statement. "That's not how it works. My family line is well documented, Mac. Every human's family is."

He frowns as he looks at me. "Every human family? What do you mean?"

I sigh. "Exactly what it sounds like. It's how we make sure humanity remains active in the world."

He doesn't say anything for a moment. Then, one lip curves up in a wry grin. "That a way for the GC to keep out the riff-raff?"

I don't answer that. I can hear the irritation in his voice, and I'm not interested in sparring with him about politics right now. "I know everything about my birth and my parent's birth and their parents' births. I know the lineage history in detail, all the way down to the hospital room I was born in. If I was a mage, there would be no hiding it. It's a matter of public record."

"Newsflash, Princess. People hide things all the time," he says. "Maybe there's something your buddies over at the GCI never told you about your life."

"Don't, okay?" I warn. "I know you're not a fan of the Cabal and their agencies. I even get that you believe you have good cause to feel as you do, but..."

I notice my fingernails are scraping relentlessly to remove the label on the nearly empty beer bottle, a nervous habit I've never been able to break, and look up, capturing Mac's eyes and willing him to understand.

"This is my life we're talking about. The GCI is more than my career. It was, it is a part of who I am."

"Is it?" he asks, raising his eyebrow. "You believe in what the Cabal does against their own people."

"The Cabal protects all the nations. Even shifters. It's not their fault that shifters are criminals."

He utters a low, hollow laugh. "Yeah, okay," he says. "Never mind the fact that reasonable people can't possibly survive under these laws. If we're criminals, it's because we have to be."

I open my mouth to respond, but I can't. I just shake my head and say, "I'm sorry you feel that way. It's not supposed to be as oppressive as you're making it sound. That's not why the Cabal was formed. We have a duty to protect the people from—"

"Save it," he says sharply, cutting me off. "If you don't get it yet that they're not the good guys—"

"Hey, they're not the ones hunting me. Bounty hunters are."

He laughs incredulously, looking at me like I've grown antlers. "You're joking, right? Somebody had to hire them. Has it even occurred to you that it might be your bosses who called those hunters on you in the first place?"

"They would never. I'm a GCI agent. I'm valuable to them."

"The hell you say," he growled. "Look, I don't know what in hell you pulled off back at your apartment or how, but I do know a human who can use magic is not a person the Global Cabal wants any more than they want a shifter who knows magic. However, if it happened, the cabal will consider a human using magic to be an abomination."

He stands and paces, his anger palpable in the air around us. "Entire neighborhoods were wiped out after the war. By the time my brother and I were old enough to serve, we'd already seen more deaths in our neighborhoods than we ever did on the field. So, don't you sit there and tell me about your benevolent employers because I promise you, if they find out what you are, you'll be tossed in a portal right beside me."

"You don't know what you're talking about," I say to him. "You don't know anything about what it's like in the Cabal. All you know is the propaganda they spread down here about it being evil. It's not evil. I'm not evil, Mac."

"You're part of the regime!" he shouts. "Whatever you might think the Cabal is, you don't understand what it's like because you're on the safe side of the gun while the rest of us are looking down the barrel! You've been sitting up in your castle so long you can't even see that they are killing us!"

I can't respond. I feel like I'm about to break down and cry for an hour. There's no energy in me to fight right now. I just can't.... "I want to be alone," I tell him. "Please leave."

The anger in his eyes dampens and I see immediate regret on his face. He doesn't argue, however. He just turns and leaves the room.

Given the heat in the room, I give him big credit for not slamming the door. I toss the empty beer bottle into the plastic bin and flop back onto the bed. My headache is back and I put one arm over my eyes to shut out the light.

My mind is spinning in circles. Mac has to be wrong, about everything. His political position is clearly indefensible, and I mentally shut that door for a long discussion another day. What keeps coming back, no matter how I look at it, is the arcane.

I. AM. NOT. A. MAGE.

This is one truth I am certain of down to my bones. But if I'm not a mage, then what in hell am I?

I open my eyes and see the ceiling. Immediately I'm reminded of how I woke up—just this morning—with my face against that very ceiling. My eyes close as if to block the memory out but it makes no difference. It was not a dream. I cannot deny this fact any longer.

And I cannot stay here any longer either.

CHAPTER TWELVE

MAC

• • • • • • • • • •

G RATEFUL FOR NOT RUNNING into anyone along the way, I weave through the tables in the bar and out the front door, still steaming from the argument. The second I step out into the cool twilight; I feel calmer. Closing my eyes, I breathe in the air, letting it chill me out for a second.

There's something about Eris lamenting about finding out she has powers that strikes a nerve with me.

I was too hard on her. I lost my family because of that stupid war and the Cabal's stupid policies. I guess it still stings more than I expected. But what the hell, where does she get off telling me the Cabal is our savior?

That's what set me off, the whole reminder of where she comes from and who she works for. I forgot who she really is. I suppose if I was a human from the GCI, I'd be conflicted, too.

"Way to go," I say into the air. I'll apologize to her later. She's probably just as steamed at me as I was at her.

Flip walks in front of me crossing the patio with an empty beer crate. I watch him carry it all the way to the trash.

As he comes back, I nod to him and shake my head "We got prospects for that kind of grunt work."

"Yeah, well, Misty's gone to see Lillian. We're short." He pulls a vape out of his pocket and starts to smoke. "Gotta call from Lillian a while ago and Misty left without barely a word. I guess she's still indebted to her or something."

"Or something."

"Anyway, I need the distraction. Still kind of shaken up from the run."

He looks like shit. Or at least like he's been in a fight, which he has. He's got a purplish bruise on his forehead and his knuckles are black and blue. He clearly didn't get it nearly as bad as everyone else did, but then Flip has a way of getting through scraps with minimal injuries. Goes back to where he got his nickname. Dire was always saying that he had a way of 'flipping the script.'

"You okay, Prez?" he asks me, tilting his head. "You look kind of worn out."

"Probably because I am worn out. It's been a rough couple of hours.

Flip nods. "Well, everybody's still here if you want to check in with the crew."

"Nah, not tonight. I've got a lot on my mind right now. Something happened with Eris that...that I don't know what to think about it just yet."

"Want to talk it out?"

I don't, really. I'm not even sure how to talk it out. Hell, I tried with Eris and ended up in a fight.

When I don't answer, Flip says, "Sometimes saying stuff out loud helps you get a better handle on it. Helps you work out the kinks, you know?"

"Yeah, yeah," I say and finish my beer. I stand there for a minute, dangling the bottle between my fingers. Finally, Flip sighs and starts back toward the door.

"She's got powers." It just slips out like a reflex or a belch. I hear Flip's footsteps stop, then start up again as he comes back.

"The girl?" he asks

I nod.

"I thought she was human."

"So did she." I pull out my own vape and take a drag. "She's having a hard time processing. She doesn't know what she is."

"Think she's part mage?"

I shake my head slowly, uncertain. I take another drag and think about it before I answer. "I don't think so," I say finally. "I mean, maybe one of her parents was a mage or something. I don't know. Flip, I saw her blast two bounty hunters through a wall with a bolt of blue fire. As if that's not odd enough, she did it when my magic was on the fritz, I couldn't fucking shift, and none of the hunters could cast a spell, either."

"Shit."

"Tell me about it. Damnedest thing I've ever seen. Up until today, I didn't think humans were capable of even knowing magic, let alone producing it."

"Well...there are people out there who don't know about us. Maybe some humans can do magic."

"Maybe. Kind of weird that she's just finding this out now, though. I mean, our powers usually come in when we're young. She's in her twenties."

"Who can say how this shit works," Flip says. "But you know, if she's a human who knows magic, then that makes her pretty unique. The Cabal will be chomping at the bit for her."

It's the very thing I'm trying not to think about and at the same time, I was trying to impress upon Eris. She is quite possibly one of a kind. A thing that's never been seen before in our history. We know all too well what the Global Cabal does with somebody like that.

"I mean...if they aren't already," Flip added. "They've gotta know about her, right? That's why the Hunters are after her. And maybe that's why we got attacked tonight. I mean, the only thing different about the run tonight was trying to get her medicine."

I look over at him and he looks back at me, standing firm in his statement. I can't deflect it. I know it's a possibility. "You think she's going to bring trouble."

"She already has, hasn't she?" Flip crosses his arms and looks out on the yard as he speaks. "Look, Prez, I'm not trying to tell you what's what, but maybe a discussion on unloading her isn't the worst idea. We can't afford an all-out war."

"No shit," I say it harsher than I mean to. "You talk about her like she's a bomb we've gotta throw over the fence."

"Isn't that what she is, though? We can handle hunters for the most part. What happens when they stop sending the hunters after her and start sending the big guns? We'd be fucked."

"Let me worry about that, all right?"

He nods, then sighs and turns to me. "Whatever you say, Prez. We need to come up with a plan soon, though. I got a feeling this last attack is not an isolated incident."

I give him a look and he nods, reading my silent message to back off. Without another word, he walks back into the clubhouse. It occurs to me I've been working a long time now without a beta. Maybe it's time to give that some consideration and Flip is looking more and more like he's ready. About damn time.

But that's not an immediate need. Right now, I just don't know what to do about Eris. I need some time to think it through. The wrong move could blow us all up.

I stand on the veranda leaning against the wall for another fifteen minutes or so before going back inside. A lot of the crew is starting to head out for the night, back to their homes to sleep in their own beds. I'm not mad at them for that. It's been a long ass night and I'm sure everybody just wants to rest up for now. I want to do the same.

But first, I need to apologize to Eris for being an asshole.

***

When I get to her door, I knock first. She doesn't answer and I feel a tight knot of worry form inside me. I open the door and see her stuffing her things in her backpack. I watch for a few seconds until she turns her head and sees me. She looks pissed. She takes a beat to glare at me, then goes back to what she's doing.

"Going somewhere?"

"I can't stay here," she says. "You and all the other shifter and mage people here are going to get me killed. I need to get back home."

I just stare at her for a moment, trying to process this logic. "Eris, if you recall, we did take you home. About forty-five minutes ago, Hunters nearly killed you. Would have killed us both, in fact."

"They tried to kill *you*." She pauses, her hand in her bag, as she turns to look at me. "I was...in the way. That's all. I've been thinking about it. If I'd been there by myself, they wouldn't have...I wouldn't have..." She closes her eyes, visibly struggling to maintain control.

Anyway, if I surrender myself—"

"Did you hit your head or something? You can't go back there!"

She whirls around, swinging her bag onto her shoulder. "I can do whatever I want. I'm not your hostage. If I want to leave, I'll leave."

As she steps around me to get to the door, I block her path. "You're not going anywhere." A deep growl escapes me. "Understand? You want to leave, you're going to have to go through me to do it and I ain't moving."

She takes a step back, looking up at me with dark, angry eyes. "So, now, you are holding me hostage."

"If that's how you want it, that's how we're doing it, Princess."

"Do not call me that. I'm not your fucking Princess."

Emotions swirl inside me as we face off. Anger, of course, I don't like to be challenged. Surprisingly, though, even stronger is a need to protect her. I lean down, getting in her face. "You're not leaving here." My tone is low, menacing. "You will stay here if I have to tie you to the fucking bed..." I pause, snarling at her. "Princess."

She slaps me and rocks my head to one side. For a pampered human, she can hit hard.

I recover quickly and before I can stop myself, I grab her by the shoulders lifting her slightly off the floor.

She pummels me in the chest with her fists as I press her close to me, restraining her.

"Let me go!" she yells. "You sonofabitch!"

"Hey!" I yell back, "knock it off!"

She manages to wiggle out of my grip, launching a haymaker straight for my head.

I lean back, avoiding it and as she stumbles, I wrap my arms around her, holding her about the waist with her back to me.

She digs her nails into my arm as she struggles. "You can't keep me here!" she shouts, kicking her legs as I lift her up.

I throw her down on the bed and before she can get back up, I wave my hands and a ring of light appears over her wrists. I lift my hands, pulling her wrists up above her head and forcing her back on the bed. She struggles and yells at me, but she's bound to the bed tight.

I look down at the scratches on my arm, trickles of blood trail down to my elbow. Shit, this is going to get infected...

"You're staying here," I say to her. Then I get closer to the bed and lean into her. "Are you hearing me right now? It is too dangerous for you to leave. You are staying here."

She grunts, yanking her arms once, twice...and then her eyes start to glow. I watch as she gives her arms another pull, breaking the ring. The magic shatters and she's free. She sits up and hits me again, slapping me across the face and chest. "I'm not your princess," she says through clenched teeth. "I'm not your fucking princess."

"All right! All right! Fuck!" I manage to grab her by the wrists, holding onto her. She twists and rises to her knees, poised on the edge of the bed as I hold her upright.

We lock eyes and in a long, charged instant there's a hum of electricity between us. I feel like the air bloomed in a single breath a thousand degrees warmer.

Her eyes flit down to my mouth and back to my eyes again. She kisses me hard.

I release her wrists, my arms moving around her waist and pulling her to me.

Her hands are in my hair and her tongue dances with mine. She gets more aggressive with her kiss, biting my lower lip hard.

The pain evokes an animal response out of me as I start to taste my own blood. My fangs and my claws are out now. I pull back, the better to see her face.

She smiles up at me, blood trailing from her mouth. Eris is playing with fire right now and she knows it. I feel her hips move and her body rub against the growing bulge in my jeans as she licks my blood from her lip. I feel her hands tangle in my hair, pulling my head down as she kisses me again.

The wolf in me is awake and threatening to show itself. Her sweet, soulful kisses are driving me to the edge. I don't know if I can hold it back.

She bites me again and this time, I push her off me and grab her around the waist, flipping her on her hands and knees. I lean into her and grab the waistband of her jeans. "You want me to make you stay?" I growl in her ear. She leans into me, arching her back as I breathe in her essence and nibble her neck.

"Yeah," she whispers. "Give me a reason."

My claws rip into her jeans, tearing them down the sides until they fall off her ass, taking her panties with them. I lean back to unzip myself and I get a view of her perfect ass, her sweet brown skin lined with claw marks from our last encounter. I slap one of her cheeks and she gasps passionately, leaning into my hand as I squeeze her firm ass.

I am rock-hard just looking at her. I lean into her, sliding myself inside her. She's so wet for me that I have to pause for a moment, a low, shuddering moan escaping my lips before I can stop it. I hold her by the hips and thrust deep, the sensation of her body and mine colliding with every dive I take.

"Oh, yeah," she moans shakily. "Fuck me hard...harder..."

I hold her tight by the hips, my claws digging into her skin. I thrust harder. She moves her hips and tightens around me as I stroke in and out. Her moans rise in timber and become raspy. The wolf inside me wants out, is pushing for the change and I push back. Mine. Eris is shivering beneath me. I feel her tighten even more around me as she climaxes, her hands pulling at the sheets as she buries her head in the pillows.

I pull out of her and push her over. "I'm not done with you yet," I growl, pulling her legs up and around my waist. I enter her again and watch as her eyes roll up into her head. I grab the collar of her shirt, pulling and tearing it free from her and exposing her breasts to me. I take a breast in one clawed hand as she sits up and kisses me deeply, my fangs piercing her lips.

Blood, sex, and magic mix between us as I hold her in my arms, thrusting deep. She moans against my mouth, her hips following my rhythm. Electricity flows between us and it feels like our bodies are humming and vibrating.

When I climax, it's harder than I have ever experienced before. I see stars before my eyes as I bury my face in her neck and stifle a howl. Her face is pressed against mine and as we kiss again, I taste her tears, her body shivering with mine as she comes with me.

"Don't let me go," she whispers. "Oh, Mac...don't let go..."

CHAPTER THIRTEEN

Eris

• • • • • • • • • • •

I T'S MORNING. THERE'S ONE window in this room and an orange light shines in and casts its rays on both of us.

Sex has never been like this before...with anyone. I wept after that first climax. Our argument devolved into passion and that into...I don't know. I'm lying here with Mac, trying to decipher what I'm feeling and I'm coming up empty. Is this love? Lust? Maybe both.

All I know is that I don't want him to leave my side. I want to be here in his arms.

His chest rises as he takes in a breath and moans. He stirs, lifting his hand to his face. I rub my hand over his chest. He takes my hand in his and holds it against his heart.

"Morning," he says.

"Morning." I nuzzle my face against his warm skin and we don't say anything to each other for a few seconds.

"That was something," he says finally. "Are you all right?"

I nod. "I think we might need to get into a first aid kit, though." My hips have been aching from his claws. Some of the scratches from the first time were starting to heal. I haven't looked, but I imagine they've all been reopened with a few more claw marks to add.

He's not unscathed, either. I left pretty deep welts in his shoulders and back and his forearm has some deep scratches, too. With our bloodied lips, I'm sure we look like we've both been in a fight.

"Sorry for getting rough," he says, then he looks at his own arm, holding it up and examining it in the light. "I guess we got carried away."

"I guess so."

He sighs, then, "Stay here. I'll be back."

He gets up and walks out of the room, stark naked. I don't know how early it is or if anyone's in the clubhouse...but he is the president. I doubt anyone will say anything if they do see him roaming around with no clothes on.

He comes back a few minutes later with one of the kits and sits on the edge of the bed. "Let's see...bandages...antiseptic...this should do just fine." He dresses my wounds, dabbing my skin gently with the cool antiseptic before pulling out the bandages.

I touch the scratches on his arm. "Jesus, these look bad."

"You put up a good fight," he says with a smile. He pauses and his smile melts away. "If I'd have let you go...you know they'd find you...right? You wouldn't stand a chance out there alone."

I don't answer him. I know he's right. I think I knew it when we started arguing.

"If something happened to you," he goes on, "I'd never forgive myself. I couldn't let you go."

I touch his face and he closes his eyes, leaning into my hand. "I guess we're in this together whether we like it or not."

His smile returns and it's brighter than the sun coming in through the window. "Yeah," he says. He presses the last bandage on the scars and looks at them for a moment before speaking again.

"So, can we talk about this for a second? The whole...magic thing?"

I pull the sheets back over my body. "I don't want to argue anymore, Mac."

"I don't either and I'm not trying to argue...but I think it's in both our best interest to give it more analysis."

I shrug. "I don't know what more there is to say."

"I think we were approaching it the wrong way," he says. "Let's try looking at this from another angle. On just the facts. That sound fair?"

I nod. "Yeah, okay."

"You're human and you can do magic. Doesn't make sense, but here we are."

I take a deep breath. I don't like it and I agree with him that it doesn't make sense...but he's right. Those are the facts as we know them. "Okay."

"We can talk about how this happened until we're blue in the face. Unless we get some more information, how are we supposed to figure it out?"

I think about that. More information. Right. That's what we need. Maybe we need someone who knows something about this...but who? I'm pretty savvy on the history of magical beings and I've never heard of this. I wouldn't begin to know where to look for information.

"Can you do something at will?" he asks suddenly.

"I...I don't know. I've never tried."

"So, try." He's sitting with his legs crossed, looking at me intensely.

I smile and chuckle. "What will that prove?"

He shrugs. "I don't know. That you can do it on purpose and if you can do it on purpose, then maybe you can learn to control it. Come on. Show me something."

I sit up, feeling embarrassed. "Like...what? I mean...I've never done it on purpose. Do you want me to try to shoot you with fire?"

"No," he laughed. "Try something safe. Like...I don't know. Levitation."

I think about waking up on the ceiling and the fall I took when I realized what was happening. I'd rather not go through that again. I shake my head. "I'll fall and break my arm or something."

"So, don't go high. Just a few inches above the bed."

"You make it sound easy."

He rubs the space between his eyes and says, "Just give it a shot. Look, I'm right here. If you get too high up, I'll pull you back down."

I purse my lips skeptically and he goes, "Trust me, Eris. I'm not gonna let you get hurt."

"Fine," I say. I lie back on the bed and close my eyes. I don't even know how it happened the first time. I was asleep, after all.

"Don't think about it," I hear Mac say. "Just feel. Feel the air around you. How cool or warm it is. Pay attention to that for a second."

I do. At first, all I feel is the warm circulation of summer that moves through the clubhouse. I realize I never questioned the comfortable temperature in this building. It's the dead of summer and this place is somewhere on the desert border and it's actually cooler in here than outside. I don't hear any air conditioning units or feel any blasts of cold air from any vents.

It's just circulating air and it's the perfect temperature. It's not too hot and not too cold. And I can hear it, a silent hissing just under the sound of everything else. I feel the air touch my skin, caressing it softly.

"I can feel it," I whisper. "It feels...I don't know...why isn't it cool?"

"Because it's not artificial air," he says, and I can hear a smile on his voice. "It's what's all around us all the time. You can feel it the strongest here because you're among mages...and nobody here wants to bake in the summer heat."

I flex my toes and I feel the air weave between the spaces. I laugh and say, "It's like it's alive."

"It is alive," Mac says. "And if you connect yourself to it, you can control it to do your bidding."

"Really?"

"Mm-hmm. So, if you wanted to float a few inches above the bed, all you have to do is tell it to lift you up." I almost laugh at that, so he adds, "Don't think about it, Eris. Just make your demand."

Don't think about it. Okay. I think only one word. Float. Before the thought is fully formed, I feel myself rising above the bed. I gasp, opening my eyes.

"Don't panic," Mac says, getting on his knees. "Just relax into it. There's nothing to be afraid of. You're in control."

I look over at him, unsure as I keep rising. "H-how do I make it stop?"

"Same way you started it. Make your demand."

I'm still rising and it's terrifying. I don't want to fall. So, don't think about it. Don't fa—

The air swishes past me as I fall back on the bed, landing in the covers. Mac leans over me, stifling a laugh.

"You okay?"

He's laughing and that's making me laugh. "Yeah," I say. "I'm fine."

Mac leans back in the bed and looks at me for a long moment. "This is a big deal, you know?

You're finding out you have powers. What you did back at the apartment...I haven't seen magic like that since the war."

He thinks for a moment, biting his nails. "What are you thinking?" I ask him.

"I'm thinking I might know someone who can help us figure this out. If anyone would know anything about something like this, it's Lillian."

The name immediately sparks my attention. I knew without him saying it who he was talking about: Lillian Ohma, leader of the resistance and public enemy number one. I used to fantasize about capturing her.

And now...now Mac is considering asking for her help. I don't know how to feel about this. It's likely she'll know who I am. Not that I'm anybody in my world. Just another pencil pusher. But I've heard the resistance is as informed about us as we are about them. It's possible I could be walking into a minefield.

"Come on," he says, getting out of bed. "We should get over there."

"Hold on a second." He pauses, looking back at me. I don't know how to say this. I swallow hard, trying to find the words.

"What? What is it?"

"Promise you'll keep me safe?" It comes out in a small voice, like a child's. I'm ashamed to sound this vulnerable.

Mac studies me for a long moment as if debating his answer. Then an odd look crosses his face, replaced instantly with a wide, reassuring smile, a decision apparently made. He sits back down on the bed and touches my face gently and my shame starts to melt even as a flame of desire sparks deep in my center.

"Already done," he says. "Let's get dressed, okay? We've got a lot to figure out and who knows how much time we have."

He's right. Who knows what awaits us today? We need to act now. We get up, shower, and dress quickly. Then he opens a portal. I take his hand and we walk through.

In the blink of an eye, we're standing in a beautiful green wood. The trees are so tall they block out the sky and everything, absolutely everything, is a vibrant green. I feel like I'm standing in the center of life itself.

"Come on," he says, pulling me out of my silent awe. "This way."

We walk down a path of soft moss and pine needles. I walk quickly to keep up with Mac, but I don't want to. I want to stay here and marvel at the beautiful forest. I didn't think there were places like this anymore. I've only seen this in pictures.

We get to a clearing dotted with a makeshift town. Huts, small buildings, and tents are arranged around an open center, like a community square or a meeting circle. A whiff of smoke rises from the glowing embers of the previous night's fire set amidst an artfully arranged pile of large rocks. So. This is the resistance. It's not at all what I thought it would look like.

A woman walks out of the largest tent and I recognize her immediately. Lillian Ohma is a shifter and head of the revolutionaries who defy the Global Cabal. A part of me feels like I'm meeting a celebrity. I've followed her exploits and studied her enough to feel as if I know her already. If I were a different person, I might ask for her autograph. As she walks up, I realize she's got no smiles for us. Her demeanor is on the offense the minute she sees me.

"So," she says, "this is the human you got mixed up with, Mac?" She raises one elegant eyebrow and turns to look at him. "I sincerely hope there's a good reason you brought an intelligence agent into this camp."

This is a mistake. I look at Mac with concern. He never should have brought me here.

CHAPTER FOURTEEN

Mac

• • • • ● • ● • • •

I CLEAR MY THROAT as Eris moves closer to me. Of course, Lillian knows who Eris is. She didn't survive this long without being able to see what's coming down the road before it reaches her.

"She's not a danger to you," I tell her. "In fact, she needs our help."

"A human employed by the Cabal does not need my help." Lillian looks from me to her. I see a flash of emerald as her eyes flash, her power engaged. "You were foolish to align yourself with her and even more foolish to bring her here, Mac."

"She's not a threat, Lillian," I repeat, raising my voice. "Look, if I was going to endanger you or this camp, I'd like to think I'd be smarter than to just walk her in through the front door."

She turns those dangerous eyes back to me...staring me down. "Why did you bring her?"

"She...she can touch the arcane. She has suddenly become able to use magic."

Lillian's face twists into an angry scowl. "Is that a joke?"

"No. I witnessed it myself. She blasted two hunters through a wall right in front of me. Saved both of our lives, truth be told."

The green in her eyes dims and she looks back at Eris. "You're...a mage?"

She shakes her head. "I'm human."

"Are you sure about that? Humans are not attuned to magic."

Eris looks up at me quizzically, then back to her. "I don't know how or why. I've never done magic before. It just...happened. For the first time, yesterday morning. I woke up to find myself floating."

"We need to understand what is happening and how," I interject. "Hunters have been after her now for a couple of days. I figure this, the magic, is why. If she's human—"

"She's not human," Lillian says. "Whatever she is, she can't be human. Earth humans do not have the ability to touch the arcane. That's not how it works."

Eris steps forward, clearly offended by us talking about her like she's not here. "Listen, have more questions than either of you, but I am absolutely sure I am human. There has never been a mage or any magical being in my bloodline."

"Sure," she says, obviously humoring Eris.

"Come on," she says to me. "We should speak privately. I have information for you."

She walks away and I see Eris scowl. "That's it?" she says. "That's all she has to say—"

I put my hand up to stop her from ranting. "Don't," I tell her as we walk behind Lillian into the compound. "Just chill until we get some answers. She will help us. There's nobody else I trust more."

Eris has plenty she wants to say. I can see it in her eyes. She's pissed Lillian has brushed her off.

"I've known Lillian a long time, Eris. There's more to this than she's said so far. Let's find out what she has to say. We'll play it her way. She's known since I first brought you into the clubhouse who you are and has no doubt had people researching everything there is to know about you."

Eris nods. Clearly not pleased, but accepting the situation for now.

In Lillian's tent, I see Misty sitting at the folding table by the boxes, a laptop in front of her. She's flipping through photos and lines of text, writing down items on a notepad next to her. She pauses long enough to greet us as we walk in.

"Hey, boss," she says, glancing at Eris.

"I was told you were summoned here," I say, then I look over at Lillian. "You know, she's our prospect, right?"

"She's solid on working with the net," Lillian says without humor. "I needed her to look into a few things for me. I'm sure you don't mind."

"Of course not," I say.

Eris steps forward, looking at the computer screen and I join her. The photo is of a man I've never seen before. He's dressed in vintage mage clothing and stands in a desert field. He's tall and dark-skinned with short-cropped white hair. He's looking off in the distance, his face a mask of determination.

"Who...who is that?" Eris asks.

Misty looks back at her, then at the computer screen. "That's Magnus Circadia," she says. "Reportedly, anyway. The photo isn't dated, and no one has claimed ownership of it. I'm trying to find a line to authenticate it."

"It's real," Eris says. Something has changed in her face. Her eyes aren't telegraphing fear anymore and she's stepping away from me as she looks at the photo from over Misty's shoulder.

Lillian turns to us. "How do you know that?" she asks Eris.

Eris opens her mouth to answer, then she closes it sharply. She frowns for a moment like she's confused or maybe unsure about whether or not she should answer. "I don't know," she says finally. "I just know it's him."

Lillian and Misty exchange glances. "Interesting," she says. "Eris, why don't you stay in here with Misty while I speak with Mac?"

She walks out of the tent, and I follow. Eris starts to go with me, but I touch her hand gently. "Stay here with Misty. I'll be right back." She nods and sits down at the table next to her.

Outside of the tent, I follow Lillian to the center of the camp where last night's fire has all but died out. I can smell the faint scent of coal and maybe some food that they had for dinner the night before. Lillian sits on the bench around the hearth, and I sit next to her.

"She's interesting," she says, "I'll give you that much."

We sit in silence for a moment, then I take a deep breath. "Lil...I need to know why she has powers. If she's human—"

"She's not human."

"You're really sure about that."

"Yes, because I understand how our magic works," she says. "Earth Humans are not genetically predisposed to handle magic in any form. I promise you, Mac. Whatever she thinks she is, whatever evidence of it she thinks she has, she's not an earth born human."

I blink at her. "So, she's a mage, then."

"At least partly. The question you should be asking yourself is not whether or not she is of mage blood, but why she believes she's a human at all."

What she's saying makes some sense and yet it doesn't. Eris is in her mid-twenties and up until a few days ago, she was working deep within the Cabal as an intelligence agent. She'd never even met a shifter before meeting me. How can she be a mage and not know it?

"In regard to the scepter," Lillian goes on, "You'll be interested to know the herb used to quell Magnus' power is called Orudis Root. It's an extremely rare plant. In its most pure form, it is considerably dangerous for mages. It shuts down our powers whenever we're in proximity to it."

I nod. "You said it didn't work with Magnus, though."

"I said it worked at first. orudis root works best when it's fresh. It loses its potency over time. My guess is whoever created the scepter didn't know enough about the plant to understand the rate of potency. I have reason to believe someone knows all about this plant and how it's used. There's evidence of it in use today, albeit covertly."

"What do you mean, covertly?"

She took a deep breath. "I think that's where the mystery of your friend comes into play. There are a few substantiated rumors of mages using the root to disguise themselves when they don't want to be tracked within the central hub. Since not every mage is an alchemist, I figured they must be getting a purified form of it somewhere. Turns out the root has been sold in medication form for years. For humans, it works as a potent, long-term pain reliever."

It clicks. The pills Eris has been taking. Except, she wasn't trying to hide her powers. She was trying to stave off migraines. Could this have been some great big accident somehow?

"There's more." Lillian pauses a moment before continuing. "In looking into your parent's murder. Mac, you should know your mother was an exceptionally powerful mage. If she had decided to serve, she would have led mage armies to greatness. It's curious, I would say unlikely even, that anyone could take her out in only one battle."

"Huh," I say thoughtfully. "Mom didn't use much magic around me and Biz. She taught us as we exhibited powers, but she was big on us keeping our magic hidden. She didn't even like it being know we could shift. It's hard to imagine her being powerful at all."

But if Lillian says it was so, I have no reason to doubt her. "So, you think this orudis root was used on her?"

"I'm 99 percent positive of it," she says. "And if that's true, given the timeline of your parent's death, whoever is responsible is probably still alive. If I had to guess? I'd say it was a human. No mage would be able to use the root against another mage without hurting themselves. The impact it has on magic is immediate and unstable."

My mind is spinning. Everything I thought I knew about what happened to my parents...was any of it true at all? I need to know more. I need to know the truth.

My phone rings, interrupting my thoughts. It's Flip. "Hey—"

"Mac! We need you back here! We're under attack!"

I hear explosions in the background, then the line goes dead. I stand up. "Gotta go," I say. "The clubhouse is under attack."

I rush back to the tent and grab Eris. "Time to go."

"What's up?" Misty says, her eyes wide.

"Clubhouse is under fire."

"Shit," she stands up to follow, but I put my hand up to stop her.

"Stay here and keep working. I need you on this right now."

She blinked. "But Mac, my place is with the club—"

"Don't argue with me. Your place is where I tell you it is. Got it?"

"Yeah. Of course."

Eris follows me as I move to the center of the tent to make a portal, and then I pause, my mind still spinning. There's no telling what we're going to find on the other side. Eris needs to be protected at all costs.

I turn to Eris, "When we go through, get to the back and hide. Don't come out unless you hear me call for you. Do you understand?"

Her eyes get large and fearful. "Mac, I--"

"Do you understand?"

She nods. "Yes...yeah. I understand."

"Good. Hold on." I take her hand and we leap through the portal. A second later, we're standing in the bar of the clubhouse. Shards of wood are flying everywhere as beams of light break through the glass and parts of the door. Flip is behind an overturned table when he sees me. "Mac!" he yells out. "Get down."

My first thought is to fight, not hide. I shift, bounding for the door and breaking it down as I leap into battle, pouncing on the first mage I see. I rip out his throat before he can react, and then I'm on another, clawing his face to ribbons.

Behind me, I hear the roars of my club, shifting and joining in the fray. We attack the mages as they throw their best magical shots at us. Having the element of surprise has helped us take down the first line, but now the second wave of mages is coming up, pushing us back by shooting blasts of white-hot fire from their hands. A few of my brothers shift back to humans and use their powers as shields, allowing us to move forward, but I can already see the tide turning. The remaining mages are about to get the jump on us.

And then everything stops. I look up to see the mages have all stiffened, hands down at their sides, as they look at us with terrified wide eyes. They're not attacking us...something is holding them...

I look back to see Eris on the patio, her eyes glowing and her hands up, holding the army of mages still. Her hands are shaking as she stands there...terrified. I shift back to human form and turn to the mages.

"Leave while you can!" I shout at them. "Or else we'll rip you apart where you stand."

I look into the eyes of each man in front of me, then I turn to Eris, hoping she's cognizant of what's happening, and nod my head to her. She lowers her hands and the mages are released. Some of them fall into the dirt, stunned for a second, but ultimately, they all scramble away, out of the yard and back across the border.

I rush to Eris. Her face is wet with tears as I pull her into my arms. "Thank you," I say, then I look down into her face. "You okay?"

She nods, but she's still shaking like a leaf. "It's okay," I reassure her. "You did good. You might've saved our asses."

"Hey, Mac!" I hear behind me. Flip and the others are looking at the fallen mages. Flip is kneeling over one, looking at him carefully.

Eris and I walk over to him and he points to the mage's hand. "Check it out."

He's wearing a ring with an insignia I've never seen before. It's gold and it has a globe with a knife through it. "So what?" I say. "He likes jewelry."

"Yeah, they all must go to the same jeweler," says Flip. "Everybody's wearing one."

I look around. Of those whose hands I can see, every mage is wearing the same ring.

"This is bad," Eris says. "Very bad."

She bites her lip as if she doesn't want to say anymore. I can feel the dread coming off her.

"Get rid of these bodies," I yell out to the crew. "When you're done, we got Church. We need to figure this shit out and now."

CHAPTER FIFTEEN

Eris

• • • • • • • • • • •

I REALLY NEED THE world to stop for at least a day and let me catch my breath. I'm a boring corporate nobody, working as an investigator because I love history and digging into old shit. What in all that's holy and I doing with a bad boy biker shifter mage and doing magic myself! If this is a nightmare, I hope I wake up soon.

Yes. Soon. Please. If this is real, how did I just save the entire Maztec biker gang? I stopped the elite of the elite in the mage world. How? How? How!

Saving them had been instinct. Mac told me to go hide, but I couldn't do it. The second I saw him rush out into battle with no thought to his own safety, I acted. I ran after him. I had to do something.

In the moments I stood watching them fight, I felt the air around me, just as I had in the bedroom. Only much more. Massive, competing eddies of energy swirled everywhere like a whirlpool. I didn't know what to do or how. My only thought was to stop the mages. I said STOP and reached out to grab their arms. I let the magic flow and said STAY, then I bound them in place, holding them down.

I stopped them. I really stopped them.

I'm so fucking scared right now. I sit in the back of the room, this sacred space reserved only for the members of the club, and I listen to them talk about what just happened. I know that I'm going to come up. I trust Mac, but I'm scared of what the others will want, and will do.

Mac is at the head of the table, mostly listening, adding a word now and then. Flip and the others talk about how everything went down. A normal morning with nothing much going on, and then out of nowhere, the mages appeared.

Mac asked if they were whole, and Flip only shook his head. I think that means that some of them have died.

I asked Mac to protect me before we left Lillian's tent. I hope he heard me. I hope, more than ever, he honors my request.

"How did they find us?" a club member asks. He's got a shock of red hair and bruises all over his face and knuckles. Some of the bruises around his eye are already starting to swell. "We've been hidden out here for the better part of a year and all of a sudden, mages attack us?"

"A better question is, who the fuck are they?" asks another. He's shorter with long, wooly hair and a beard covering most of his face. "I mean, those were definitely not Hunters. They were fucking organized."

"Military," said Flip. "Obviously from the Cabal." He looks at Mac as if expecting him to say something. He doesn't. He just looks across the room to me. And everyone's head turns.

I guess here is where I add my two cents.

"They were wearing rings with the High Council insignia etched," I say softly. "It's...it's the highest court in the land. The high council make the laws, send out the judgments on who gets imprisoned or banished. Those mages were clearly from the high council's personal army. They call themselves The Corps."

My words hit them like a wave, a ripple of reactions from every man at the table. Flip is the first to speak up. "You're shitting me, right?"

"No," I say, clasping my hands to keep them still. "No, they...they're real. But...but..." God, I don't want to say anymore. I feel like such a fucking fool right now.

"Go on," I hear Mac say. I look up at him and though he's not smiling at me or offering any encouragement other than his words, I feel his invisible hand of protection on me.

"The Corps doesn't do what they just did," I tell them. "There...there are no records of the corps armies just...showing up and attacking unprovoked. I've only ever found one incident where they were brought in to calm a violent area of unrest..."

"Like in the Lupin district about twenty or thirty years ago?" the short, hairy one says. "The one where all the shifters were wiped out except Dire? Like that?"

Mac gives him a look and he backs off, shaking his head and looking back down at the table. "All I'm saying," he continues, "is if the Authority is sending their big guns our way, it must be for a pretty damn good reason."

I see Flip look at Mac, tapping his fingers on the table nervously. The action doesn't go unnoticed by anyone else. The hairy one is glaring at Flip angrily.

"Say it plain," Mac says. "You got something on your mind, Jake. Let's hear it."

Jake looks at Mac, then says, "Seems to me a human who can do magic might be kind of a big deal to the authority. Something they might want to send hunters after and when that doesn't work, they come in and kick the door down themselves."

My mouth has gone dry. I don't like where this conversation is going. Mac says, "So, what are you suggesting? Do you want to throw our guest to the wolves? Send her off so that they'll leave us alone? That's what you want to do?"

"I didn't say that," said Jake. "I'm just saying—"

"I know what you're saying," Mac said, a sly smile appearing on his face. "You want to turn tail and run like a bitch. Toss the human on the fire and split...right?"

Jake doesn't respond and I feel the entire mood of the room shift. Mac's in control of the room now.

"We don't offer up sacrifices to the Authority," he says. "We don't hurt the innocent and we don't negotiate with terrorists. If the Cabal is after Eris, then that makes her valuable and worthy of protection from us. Get it? Because if any of you don't, then maybe you're working for the wrong side."

"Mac," says the redhead. "Nobody's saying nothing like that. Look, they got three of our guys and they might've wiped us all out completely. What happens when they come back here?"

"That's not going to happen because we won't be here," Mac says. "And even if they do come back before then, we'll beat them back again. What part of that don't you understand? We're Maztecs. We stand against the Cabal. We will do nothing to aid them. Ever. Am I clear?"

They agreed in unison. Mac absolutely had the room now.

"They now know where we are. We won't give them another chance at us until we've built up our resources. Gather your shit. We're heading to Lillian's camp as soon as possible. Alpha protocol. Family and essentials only. No goodbyes. No warning to anyone outside of the family. You all know the drill."

He slams down the gavel to end the meeting and the men and women disburse fast. I watch them go. Mac is still at the table, thinking.

"Mac...?"

"Get your things," he says. "We need to leave as soon as everyone's ready."

***

We've been riding for hours. The sun has long set and I'm trying to stay awake so I don't fall off the back of the bike. Riding with Mac is the most calming experience I've ever had. The vibration of the bike under me; the changing of the desert around us to the lush green trails of the enclosed wood where the camp is hidden; the feel of my arms around Mac and the smell of leather as I rest my head on his back; combine to make me feel calm and protected.

He's keeping his promise to make sure I'm safe. I'm not sure if it's because it's the right thing to do or if he has some affection for me. I'd like to think the latter is true, given our sexual connection. I hope there's more between us. There certainly seems to be.

The bike slows down as we weave through the thick wood. We get to the clearing and once again, Lillian stands out front, waiting for us with Misty at her side. Mac backs the bike into a parking area and then helps me down. My legs are like rubber and I'm glad for the assist as I would surely have fallen without his arms holding me up as my legs decided to hold me up.

"You'll all be staying in the main hut," Lillian says when the collection of bikes and cars are parked and the majority standing behind Mac and me. "Misty will show you the way."

Misty takes us to a building more solid than most of the makeshift huts and tents all around us. It's made from rock and mortar, and inside, there have been walls erected from logs of wood. We walk into the first large room with couches and chairs, and then Misty directs us down a hallway where there are other rooms, all connected through two adjoining hallways.

Mac and I share a room near the center of the structure. I imagine that's strategic. We're the most protected if someone should attack us. The room is incredibly spacious, with a large, king-sized bed in the center. The frame is made of wood and as I press down on the mattress, I hear the soft crinkle of what feels like leaves or moss under the heavy fabric.

"This is amazing," I say to Mac. "They really made a home here."

Mac nods. "Lillian has been trying to find someplace permanent for everyone to stay. It's more of a pipe dream than anything, but...everywhere she chooses has these semi-permanent structures in them. Some of them they build, and some are already there. It's her way of looking for her home, I think."

That makes me smile. At the moment, I can relate.

"I need to speak with Lillian for a moment. Why don't you go ahead and get some sleep? I'll try not to wake you when I return."

Weariness is quickly overwhelming me and I nod in agreement. In only a few minutes, I sink down into the softness of the bed and drift off to sleep almost instantly.

***

Something wakes me. A sound? A movement of the bed? Not sure. I roll over, my hand reaching out to Mac. When I don't feel anything, I sit up and see him in a chair at the far end of the room. He's got an old notebook in his hands and he's reading from it, turning the pages slowly.

"Mac?" I say and he looks up at me. "What are you doing up? Is everything okay?"

"Yeah," he says. "Everything's fine. Honest. Go on back to sleep."

He doesn't look right. Even in the dim of this room. He looks...well, like he's been crying. He wipes at his face and gets up from the chair, putting the notebook down and heading to the bathroom. He's shirtless, wearing only his boxers.

Now he's up and he looks agitated. I get up and follow him. In the bathroom, which is a curtained square in one corner of the room, he's leaning over the sink (which is a bucket with water in it). He splashes the water on his face.

"You're not okay," I say.

He looks up at me, water dripping into his eyes and down his face. He takes a minute and rubs a towel over his eyes. "Let me show you something."

He leads me out of the bathroom and to the chair where he left the notebook. "This," he says as he picks it up, "is my brother's journal. It's the last thing of him that I have left, other than the necklace you returned to me."

He walks over to the bed and pats the mattress, inviting me to sit. "I told you my parents were killed." He opens the book and spreads it between us on the bed so that both of us can see. "Murdered. They came to our home, and they killed my mother. We were hidden when it happened. In the storm cellar under our house. I didn't see anything, but Biz, he saw it all."

I watch him flip through the pages, waiting, listening intently. I can tell this is a story he does not share. It hurts, even now many years later.

"You'd think Biz would want to tell me what happened, but he always refused to talk about it. Instead, he wrote it all out here. Except he put everything in code. It's all...all just clues. Clues that I've been trying to figure out all this time."

He sighs, and then he closes the book. "We were just kids when they were killed. We didn't know anything about anything. We understood the mage army was involved somehow. That's why we joined the war effort. We thought maybe if we got trained to kill mages, maybe we'd get the ones that killed our folks."

I lean into him, resting my head on his shoulder. "Turns out it wasn't mages," he says. "That's what I found out when we were here earlier. Not mages. Couldn't have been."

He touches his necklace, rubbing his fingers over the smooth amber. "The bullet in this necklace I dug out of him myself," he says. "Thought if I could get it out...I could save him. Burned the shit out of my fingers doing it." A single tear wells up in his eyes and rolls down his cheek. "He didn't have to die, Eris. We joined the war to fight mages...but it wasn't them that did the killing. We didn't have to die."

"Your brother, he didn't know either? You said he saw—"

"I don't know if he knew it wasn't mages," he says. "He knew the scepter was involved, though. He didn't know how I think, but..."

He trails off. I don't fully understand what he's getting at with the scepter or its connection to his parent's death, but I don't think that's the point. That's only part of it.

His fingers are still circling the amber around his neck. "He joined the war because I did," he whispers. "He never would have thought to do it if I wasn't hell-bent on finding our parent's killers. It...it was all for nothing."

My heart is aching for him. I reach over and touch his face, turning it to me. "You couldn't have known," I say. "However it happened, you could never have known." I wipe away another tear with my thumb and he leans into me, resting his forehead against mine with closed eyes.

"The entire trajectory of my life could have been different," he says. "We might both be here right now..."

I lean in and kiss him, my lips pressing against his lovingly. I can't take away his pain. I can't bring his brother back. But maybe I can show him that I care. Let him forget his pain for a while...

CHAPTER SIXTEEN

MAC

• • • • • • • • • •

I KISS HER BACK, first gently sucking her lips, then her tongue dances with mine. I lean into her, my hand on her thighs and moving up to her waist. Our lips part and I look into her eyes, a silent communication flying between us. As I pull up her shirt, she helps me, getting it over her head and tossing it across the room.

Topless, she straddles me. I take hold of her breasts, kissing them gently, then letting my tongue roam along her skin and around her hardening nipples. I take my time with her, caressing and sucking on them while she moves her hips back and forth against my growing erection pressing against her panties. She's so wet right now, I can feel it through her panties and my boxers. I grab hold of her ass, squeezing as she rubs her clit against me with nothing but the fabric of our underwear between us.

I move my hands up her back, bracing her as I roll her onto the bed. I kiss her body, moving down to her navel, my warm tongue traveling down to her hips. I pause to pull off my boxers, then I return to kissing her sweet thighs as I reach for her panties, slipping my fingers between the fabric and sliding against the folds of her sex, enjoying the warm wetness of her body.

She shudders under my touch, eager for me. I slip two fingers inside her and watch as her eyes roll to the back of her head. She bites her lip, small, shaky moans escaping her lips.

She's so fucking hot and I'm so hard for her right now. I stop my finger work and I pull off her panties, sliding them down her thighs. I lower myself down between her legs and they shiver against me in anticipation. I grab hold of her thighs, keeping her stable as my tongue meets her sweet, wet center. She grabs hold of my head, her fingers running through my long hair. I hold her close, exploring her with my tongue.

"Don't   stop,"   she   whispers. "Oh...Mac...don't...oh!" She comes against my tongue, her legs shaking in my arms. I keep going, sucking on her clit as her moans rise in pitch.

"Fuck..." she cries out, her back arching. I release her, running my hand over her smooth skin. She's panting. I watch her beautiful breasts move up and down rapidly as she catches her breath.

The last two times we were together were kind of rough and almost rushed in nature. Explosions of tension that's been building between us. Not this time, though. This time, I want to journey with her. I want to feel her heart beating with mine. I want us to be joined in every way that matters.

I move between her legs and enter her, kissing her deeply as I dive in. We moan in time with one another as I thrust slowly and methodically. She lifts her legs and I dive deeper. She feels like heaven to me. Her body is a divine temple. The one place on this earth where I can be safe and pure. She moves her hips with mine, throwing back her head and moaning as I bury my face in her neck.

No fangs this time. The wolf in me sleeps, as content to be with her as I am to be here. She kisses me again, tightening herself around my cock. I'm so close I feel like I'm going to go any moment. I kiss her neck and she runs her hand through my hair. The urge to mark her starts within me. My tongue runs along her shoulder.

I stop myself, pulling myself up and stiffening my arms. I hope she doesn't notice. I close my eyes, focusing on just the sexual part of this. I feel her hands on my face.

"Hey," she says in a whispery tone. "Stay with me."

I open my eyes and we connect again. My heart is pounding like a drum. The animalistic urge to make her mine almost overwhelms me.

I can't. She doesn't know what it means...a mark is forever...

I feel her wrap her legs around my waist and she pulls me into her again. My arms go weak as she kisses me again. "I love you," she whispers. "Oh, Mac...I love you..."

I love her. God, help me, I do. I love this woman...

"Mark me," she whispers.

I pause, thinking I didn't hear her right. I look into her eyes. She...knows? "Eris," I whisper. "Do you understand what that means?"

"It means I'm yours," she says. "I don't know how this will end, Mac...but I know I belong with you."

I'm stunned. She understands. She leans her head to the side, exposing her neck and shoulder to me. My fangs come out automatically.

"Make me yours," she says.

I can't hold back from her now. I lean into her shoulder, feeling her warmth against my lips...and I bite into her. The taste of blood fills my mouth as I thrust into her. She gasps, her nails digging into my back.

She starts to shake in my arms and the feel of her body climaxing, the taste of her blood in my mouth...it's too much...

I explode inside her, thrusting hard as my grip on her tightens. Her moans are loud and shaky and I have to let her go. As I release her, a hard and husky howl escapes me. Stars flash in front of my eyes as

I climax, the energy within me flows into her and back.

And when the wave leaves me, I lean my head against her, the taste of her blood still in my mouth.

"I love you," she whispers.

"I love you," I whisper back.

I bandage up her shoulder, then we sleep for the rest of the night. Lying with her in my arms feels right, like it's always been this way or should have been. Always me and her...

Is this Celestia? Is this the legendary thing that binds lovers to each other for eternity? I don't know. I told Dire about it, but this didn't happen like it did for Dire. He was compelled to be with the love of his life. I don't feel...compelled as much as I feel this is meant to be.

***

It's morning already and Eris is sound asleep. I need to figure things out for the club. There are decisions to be made.

There's a knock at my door. "Hey, Mac? You decent?"

Eris stirs. I don't want to wake her, so I slip out of bed and grab my boxers on the floor before going to the door. When I answer, Misty stands on the other side, wearing a crop top and blue sweatpants...and no kutte. I swear, she's gotta be the worst Prospect we've ever had.

"Where's your kutte?" I ask her.

"In my room. It's early. I haven't even showered yet."

"I don't care. You don't get an audience with me without it and you know that."

She sighs. "It's important, Mac. I wouldn't have come to your door if it wasn't. It's about Magnus Circadia."

"Okay, what about him?"

She pauses, looking down at her feet briefly. "I think maybe both of you ought to hear about this."

"Fine. Let us get dressed and we'll talk."

I close the door and turn to Eris, still asleep in bed. Lillian had hinted that our fates might be intertwined. Maybe what Misty's found is the missing piece that links us together.

I wake her and we shower together...which almost turns into another round of sex. I'm eager to find out what Misty found, though, so I stave off Eris' affections, which isn't an easy task. But we have to focus. We need to do whatever we can to get on the other side of all this.

Showered and dressed, we go to Misty's room. Misty (wearing her kutte this time) pulls out her laptop as she sits at the desk by her bed.

"So," she starts, "you guys remember this photo, right?" She pulls up the picture of Magnus standing in a field.

"The picture that you don't know anything about who took it?" I say and she nods.

"Right. Well, this photo is found in an old archive. It was buried deep in the net. Like in a digital slush pile. So, I had to track where it came from. Turns out this is one of about a hundred family photos from an old, discarded album."

She clicks the screen and a bunch of photos come up in a list. "Family photos?" Eris asks. "Who's family?"

"Magnus' apparently," she says. She clicks on one of the photos. Magnus with a young woman, dark-skinned like him with long curly hair. He's wearing a suit and tie and she's in a wedding gown. But that's not the surprising thing. I look at the woman and see it immediately.

I don't say anything at first. I just look at Eris. Her face dips into a deep frown. "He had a wife?" she asks.

Misty nods and moves to the next photo. Magnus and the woman are at a party. They're standing in front of a fireplace with wine glasses in their hands, a happy moment captured between them. Standing around them were five children of varying ages. Including one small child in Magnus' arms.

"Children," Eris whispers.

"Yup."

She shakes her head in confusion. "He...he didn't have children. There are no records of Magnus being married or...or having children. This doesn't make sense."

"Are you sure this is Magnus?" I ask Misty.

"That's the thing. I didn't have any confirmation other than Eris saying it is. But then, I found this." She closes the folder and opens up another one, opening a document. At the top, the heading reads, Order of Execution.

"Execution...?" Eris says. "I don't understand."

Misty looks at me as if asking for my permission to continue. I nod and she takes a deep breath, turning the laptop back around.

"'This order calls for the execution of one Magnus Circadia'," she reads, "'Loris Circadia, Olana Circadia, Melonius Circadia...'"

"Wait, wait." Eris' eyes had gotten large. "Who...who are all they? He didn't have any family—"

"Eris—" I reach out to her and she pushes me away.

"No. I know his history. I know it better than I've known anything else. He did not have a family. And if he did...if he did, why would they kill them? He was a hero."

Misty is watching us both carefully. I take Eris by the hand and lead her to sit down on Misty's bed. "Let's reserve judgment, okay?" I say to her. "We don't know everything yet." I look to Misty. "What else did you find?"

"Well," she says, setting the laptop back on her desk, "the thing is…Well, I found their death certs. They were also buried in the slush pile. Loris was his wife and the others were all his children."

Eris shakes her head in disbelief. "So…the story of Magnus Circadia is a lie?"

Misty nods and she looks over at me again before she says the rest. "The authority ordered their execution once the war was won," she said. "He and most of his family were executed in their home."

"Most of his family?" I ask and she nods again.

"The youngest child was never found. An infant, maybe toddler age, a girl named Alura."

I feel my stomach drop. I'm adding it all up. What Lillian told me about Magnus and how he was betrayed. The fact that it was probably someone of non-magic origin, possibly a human, who created the scepter to quell his power. Possibly, the same person who killed my parents. A human who used Orudis Root, maybe using the scepter, to weaken my mother...

But this...this was something different. Something so much bigger than I ever thought we'd find. He had a family. Five children...and a wife...a wife who looks just like...

I look at Eris, who is looking back at me in complete confusion. She doesn't see it. How could she? She doesn't have the other pieces to the puzzle. How can I tell her?

"I don't..." she pauses and laughs, nervously. "I don't get why we need to know this. What does Magnus Circadia have to do with anything that's happening now? Is this about the Scepter somehow?"

She has to know. I have to tell her. Her life has already been turned upside down. What will this do to her?

The door opens to Misty's room. It's Flip. "Oh, great, you're in here," he says when he sees me and Eris. "A message just came over the net that you two ought to see."

It'll have to wait, I realize. "Come on," I tell Eris.

We all get up and follow Flip out of the room.

We walk into the front room where Lillian and the others are gathered around a large monitor hanging on the wall. Two humans are visible, standing together against a white wall. A man and a woman, holding hands. The man is brown-skinned with round wire-rimmed glasses and the woman is slight, small-boned with angular features like a bird.

"Oh, my God," said Eris. "It's my parents."

The video starts and the man speaks, "To the people holding my daughter Eris hostage. She is a wonderful, sweet, and intelligent woman and is our only child. We beg of you to please release Eris. We only want her safe return..."

"It's been circulating for the last hour," Lillian says, her arms crossed. "It's made the news and most of the central hub has been buzzing about it." She looks over her shoulder at us. "Everyone's looking for you."

Eris doesn't respond. She watches the video in silence, clearly unable to take her eyes off the screen.

"We do not want to pursue any action against you," her father says, "We only want our daughter back. If you reach out to us directly, we will be willing to negotiate her release."

"Turn it off," I say.

Eris whips her head around to me. "Mac, they're worried about me. I've been missing for a few days now."

"I don't trust it," I say. "Something's off about it."

Eris implores me, her brown eyes large and pleading. "They're my parents, Mac. What do you expect them to do? They're terrified for me. I should reach out to them. Let them know I'm all right."

"Not a chance," I say with a laugh.

"Mac—"

"This is a trap! They're trying to lure you out into the open. We can't take a chance—"

"*They* are my parents. Look, I know you're distrustful of humans, but we're not all bad. Some of us are good people."

It's like she punched me in the stomach. "I know that, but this is obviously a trap."

"Why would you think that? It's just a phone call. We can take precautions."

Everyone's looking at us now. Wondering which way this is going to turn and for good reason. We just fucking got here.

"One phone call," I say. "And you'll make the call in another location. Understand?"

"Yes. Thank you, Mac."

I walk away in search of a burner phone. I hope I don't regret this.

CHAPTER SEVENTEEN

Eris

• • • • **•** • **•** • • •

T HE PROCESS OF CALLING my father involved Mac getting a burner phone and portalling me to another location. Where we were was more desert than land, surrounded by old, burned-out buildings. As soon as we got there, he said, "Five minutes. That's it."

What I'm going to say to him? That I'm in love with Mac? I don't know how that's going to fly. That I can suddenly perform magic? I do know that won't fly. I can't talk to my father about either. For now, I'll tell him that I'm all right. And that I'm not kidnapped.

I dial his number. It rings three times before he picks up. "Hello?"

"Dad?"

There's a gasp, then, "Eris? Oh, my God. Is it really you?"

"Yes, it is," I tell him. "I saw your press conference and I just wanted to tell you that I'm okay."

"Oh, thank God. You're not being mistreated, are you?"

"No. I'm being treated well, actually. I just wanted to call to tell you not to worry. I haven't been kidnapped. I'll be...away for a while and will let you know when I'm ready to come home."

"Honey, I'm so glad you're okay." He sounds like he's crying. "Your mother and I are worried. You didn't show up for work, and you weren't at home... Everyone has been looking for you. The entire town has been searching the streets for you. Where are you?"

"I'm safe. That's all I can say for now."

"When can I see you? Darling, when are you coming home?"

The hurt in his voice weighs on me. My father is worried, and I can't blame him. From his perspective, his only child has disappeared. I can't imagine how much terror and stress he must be experiencing.

"Dad, I can't come home just yet. It's...complicated. I need to stay here. I want to stay here. There's a lot going on and I need to see this through."

"I don't understand, sweetheart. Will you at least meet with me? Somewhere public. We can have coffee—"

"Dad, I can't."

"Please, Eris. I need to know you're okay. Have you been taking your medicine? Do you need a refill? You should still be taking it while you're away. Let's meet so I can give it to you."

I wish I could tell him everything. Maybe he wouldn't be worried about me if he could see me in the flesh.

"It can be in public," he says. "You remember Lalo Park? Just outside the central hub? We used to go there when you were little."

I glance over at Mac, who's pointing at his watch. "Dad, I have to go."

"Just meet me there. Tomorrow morning after ten. I'll be there waiting for you."

I hang up and I bite my lip thoughtfully. He just wants to see me. What could the harm be?

"Okay," Mac says, "Let's go."

"Wait. I...he wants to see me."

Mac just stares at me. "So?"

"Mac...he's my father. I should go and see him."

He sighs and shakes his head. "He thinks you've been kidnapped. If you go, he'll probably find a way to make you stay."

I laugh. "First of all, I'm an adult. He can't make me do anything I don't want to do. Look, you can just portal me there. I'll find a way back."

"You're kidding, right? You think you can just hop a cab back here?"

"Could you not be a smart ass about this? Look, it's important he knows I'm okay and I'm not being held hostage."

He just stares at me.

"It won't be for long and it'll be in a public place. I'd be gone an hour tops. You could portal me there and then open a portal to bring me back. No problem."

He crosses his arms, studying me thoughtfully. "Fine, you can go, but I'm coming with you."

The idea of my father meeting Mac sends rivulets of terror through me. He would not approve of him.

"Mac—"

"This isn't a debate, Eris. Either I go along or you stay here. You are not going alone."

He seems wired up about something. Like there's a risk if I go alone. "It's just my Dad. You think I need protecting from my own father?"

"It's better to err on the side of caution. We're clearly in uncertain times."

"Okay," I say. Both of us go.

"Fine. Tomorrow morning at ten." He nods. Then he turns and opens a portal.

As we're about to step through, I take his hand, then I stand on my tiptoes and kiss him gently. "It'll be fine," I say to him. "You'll see."

"I hope you're right."

***

Mac's been quiet all morning. He's been keeping to himself like there's something on his mind. I wonder if he's having trouble talking about it? I don't know why he's suddenly so distant. I hope he's not pissed at me for wanting to see my dad.

Maybe he thinks that I'm going to leave and never see him again. I guess that's a reason for him to worry. He believes my father will say or do something that will compel me to stay, which is ridiculous of course.

I'm not going to go with my dad, though. I love Mac and whatever happens from this point on, he's the man in my future.

He comes out of the bathroom, dressed in his kutte, blue jeans and a black t-shirt. He's tying his hair back in a ponytail as he looks up at me. "Ready?"

I want to talk to him about this. Maybe reassure him I'm not going anywhere, but there's no time. It's almost ten o'clock. "Yup," I say instead.

He nods and opens the portal.

We walk through. Mac has clearly been here before. He's put the portal behind an old maintenance building across the street from the park. It's ten, so it's peak time for people to be there and a portal appearing in the middle of the park would surely freak out everyone.

There are people walking along the trails and several joggers running along the track circling the park. There are even a few people with children playing by the pond near the entrance.

Mac stands next to me, scanning the street silently. "What are you looking for?" I ask him.

"Trouble," he says simply. "I meant what I said. The first sign of anything fishy and we're out of here."

"Got it," I say. "Can I go inside now?"

He nods. "I'll stay out here and stand watch."

He's standing there with his arms crossed, looking through the gate across the street. "I'll be right back," I tell him. "I just want to talk to Dad. Thirty minutes. Tops."

He opens his mouth to say something, then he stops himself and plasters a smile on his face instead. "I'll be here whenever you come out. Be careful."

I take his hand and squeeze it, then I make my way across the street and through the high, gated entrance. I don't see Dad...oh, wait. There he is. Sitting by the pond.

I jog over to him and the minute he sees me, he stands up, his eyes wide with delight. I run into his arms, hugging him warmly.

"Eris," he says, holding me tight. "Thank the heavens, you're all right."

"Of course, I'm all right," I say as he lets me go. He looks at my face, taking it in his hands for a moment.

"You look thin," he says. "Did they torture you? Starve you?"

"I wasn't kidnapped, Dad," I say to him. "I was just away for a while, that's all."

"Away? Without telling anyone? Where have you been?"

I smile and take his hands. "It's kind of a long story. Maybe I can tell it another time."

We sit down on the bench together and for a moment, this feels like when I was a child. Dad used to take me to this pond to feed the ducks.

"So, I don't get to know where you've been. Is it some great secret?"

"No," I laugh. "I mean...it's complicated, that's all."

He nods. "Well...I'm glad you're all right. I was thinking now that you're back, you should probably stay with us for a while. Just until you can get reacclimated."

I blink at him. Did he not hear me just now? "I'm fine, Dad," I say. "Like I said, I wasn't kidnapped at all. Look, can we talk about something else? How's Mom?"

He nods, pushing his glasses up on his nose. "Better now she knows her daughter is alive and well. She looks forward to seeing you again."

I smile at him. He wants me to come back home. I can't blame him, really. He just wants to make sure I'm okay. He rests a hand on my knee and I freeze.

The ring he's wearing. I don't know that I've ever seen it before now. It's gold with the insignia in the shape of the world with a knife in it.

I can't process this. It's a High Council ring. Why...why is he wearing it?

"When we get you home, it'll be all right again," He reaches into his pocket and hands me a glass jar. My pills. "Since you've probably been without them all this time. I know your migraines must have been terrible."

"Thank you," I'm confused. My father has never been a member of the high council. Why does he have that ring?

"I should go," I say to him. "I have to get back."

I stand up and he takes me by the hand. "I don't think so."

I tilt my head, looking at him in confusion. As I open my mouth to ask what he means, we are suddenly surrounded by Authority agents.

CHAPTER EIGHTEEN

MAC

• • • • ● • ● • • •

E VERYTHING ABOUT THIS IS a setup. I feel it in my bones. Leaning against the park gate's ornate metal frame, neither in nor out, I stick out like a black sheep in the middle of the herd. There is no way I'm leaving her, though so I scan the park and the busy street both, watching for anything suspicious, anyone taking note of Eris and her father.

She's wrong about him. I can't let go of the belief that coming here was a mistake. He is not going to let her leave with me. He has a plan to compel her to stay with him. Nothing else makes sense.

All morning, I've been putting together the possibilities in my mind. How did Eris come to be with the people she calls her parents? They had to have adopted her. Taken her in once her family was killed. But with all of her research experience, how could the adoption not be a part of her records?

They never told her what she really is, I get that. They suppressed her powers and kept her hidden in the human world. I can think of a million reasons why humans might do that...and honestly, they're all varying degrees of bad, bad, and bad. I've never known humans to be particularly benevolent when it comes to any of us. Sure, they allow Mages to roam more freely than shifters, but all supernaturals are second-class citizens in this world.

Humans are at the top of the food chain. What would they want with the child of a mage?

A part of me wants to be as optimistic as she is. I suppose that's why I agreed to this ill-advised meeting. I want to believe this is simply a father wanting to see his daughter.

I hope to God that's all this is. They'll talk. She'll come back to me, and we'll leave.

And yet, I know I'm lying to myself. I wasn't born yesterday. I know a setup when I smell it and the reek of trap is undeniable here.

Her father hands her a glass jar, no doubt her medicine, and she stands.

I take a step away from the gate, my full attention focused on Eris now.

"Excuse me, sir."

Two men step in front of me, blocking the sidewalk. They flash badges, not that the shields were needed, they couldn't be more obviously Authority. Tweedle Dee and Tweedle Dum. Uh-oh.

"We need you to come with us," Tweedle Dee says.

"I don't think so." I can still see Eris and she's in trouble. Fuck. I really hate being right.

"Listen," he continues, holding out his hands as if to say he's harmless. *Bloody hell.* "...we can do this the easy way or the hard way. If it's all the same to you, we don't want to make a scene. Why don't you come quietly?"

More agents have surrounded Eris. She yanks her arm away as one grabs her. They're going to take her...

The other agent, Tweedle Dum, makes a grab for me and I sidestep, grabbing his arm and yanking him forward until he stumbles and falls. I kick him down and his face slams against the concrete. Suddenly, half a dozen more come out of nowhere, punching and kicking at me.

One of them shoots a ring bolt in hopes of binding me. I dodge it and them, shifting into a wolf in mid-stride as I run for Eris, being herded toward the entrance by a pair of agents.

No! I leap, knocking one agent down and away from her.

Eris stumbles back, punching at the one still holding her. He grabs her by the wrist and twists her arm around her back.

Her father yells, "Get her out of here!"

He's standing, pointing at her. It's then I see it. He's wearing a High Council ring. The same ring we found on dead mages after they attacked us.

Sweet Jesus. That's the missing piece. I was right to trust my instincts about him. I need to get Eris out of here now.

I turn to attack the one holding her, and a white-hot pain shoots through my shoulder. The impact pushes me backward and forces me to change back to human form. Tendrils of smoke rise from the wound. My kutte is torn and burned, and filling up with blood.

Silver. Probably a bullet. Maybe a dagger. Whatever it is, I'm bleeding buckets now. As I scramble to my feet, I taste metal in the back of my throat. That's not good.

"Mac!" Eris screams as they lift her off her feet and carry her off.

I can't go after her. Goddammit!

...the pain...

They're closing in on me. I have no choice but to retreat. I have to live long enough to find her again.

I wave my hand and summon a portal.

The last image I see as I fall backward through the portal is burned into my memory; the faces of the Authority agents closing in on me drain of all color, stunned by my use of portal magic. In the background, Eris is being carried away as her father glares at me, triumph and hate clearly legible.

The second I hit the floor in Lillian's living room, black filled with tiny specks of stary white envelopes my sight.

"Shit, I need help over here!" Lillian says. With the last bit of consciousness, I see her face lean in close to mine….

CHAPTER NINETEEN

ERIS

• • • • • • • • • •

IT'S BEEN FOUR DAYS. Four days since they shot Mac and dragged me back to my parent's house.

The big showdown in the park has been the lead story on every newscast the whole week. A shifter using magic to escape. And someone got it all on a cell phone camera.

God, I hope he's okay. I hope he's still alive.

I wish I could stop thinking about him. I haven't left my room except to eat since I've been back. Dad insisted I stay with him and Mom, saying the kidnappers might look for me at my house. I've given up trying to convince them I was with Mac and the others of my own free will. They don't believe it anyway.

In fact, last night at dinner, Dad suggested I make an appointment with a therapist to discuss what happened. Since, you know, I'm not talking to them about it.

I don't know what to say. I'm upset about what they did, although a part of me understands. They believe I was kidnapped after all. They thought they were capturing my abductor.

I suppose I should be thankful for that kind of love and protection. There are people who would let their children run loose and never bother to go look for them. At least my parents thought to do something about getting me back.

Yeah. I suppose I should be grateful.

Oh, who am I kidding? I'm not okay with this. I miss Mac. More than that…I was so close to figuring out this whole magic thing I've got going on. I think it's got something to do with Magnus Circadia. I've got an idea that fits, but there's a piece missing in my theory that I just can't fill in.

I've been thinking about what Misty found and why she thought it was important to tell us both about it. I don't exactly know what Circadia could have to do with me, but since Mac stole his Scepter and Mac believes it was used to kill his parents, it makes sense he should know what she finds.

How did I know it was him when I saw that first photo of him? I can't explain it. The second I saw it, I knew it was him, even though it didn't really look like any other picture I'd ever seen of him. Maybe that's part of the magic somehow.

Speaking of magic, I've been trying to do magic since I got back, but it doesn't seem to be working now. It's like I've shorted out somehow. Every night before I go to sleep, I close my eyes and try to feel the magic around me, but I don't feel anything. It's like a light switch has been turned off in my mind.

I look out of my bedroom window and think of Mac. If I close my eyes, I can almost smell him. The scent of leather and sweat. If I imagine hard enough, I can feel his hands on my body. I wish he was with me right now. How I miss being in his arms and feeling his lips on mine.

He said he would protect me and to his credit, he did his best to do just that. And they shot him for it. He looked so bad...there was so much blood.

Please let him be okay. Please. Let him be alive.

There's a knock at my door. "Dinner's ready, sweetheart." It's my mother. I suppose I should eat. I get up and pass by a mirror, pausing the second I see it.

The mark on my shoulder. Mac's mark on me. It's scabbed over, but it's healing well. Mother almost fainted when she saw it. Luckily, she hasn't seen the scars on my hips.

I touch it and the sore spots shoot lightning bolts of pain through my arm. It's painful...but it's a good pain. It reminds me of Mac.

I leave my room and walk down the stairs to dinner. I get about halfway when I hear my name. I slow down, listening.

"I think you're worrying too much about her." It's my father talking. "Our daughter is a strong and intelligent woman. She'll bounce back from this."

"Maybe," Mom says. "I just worry that she's got permanent damage from what's happened to her.

She was gone for days with those animals. There's no telling what they did—"

She stops abruptly as I walk the rest of the way down the stairs. They look up at me through the archway of the dining room. Father smiles at me, taking his napkin and unfolding it onto his lap.

"Finally," he says. "I'm starving."

I sit down in my seat next to Dad and across from Mom. My plate has already been made out for me and is sitting in front of me. Just like it was when I was a girl. Nothing ever changes around here.

"I hope you had a good rest," Mom says. "You've been through quite an ordeal."

I don't say anything to that. I unfold my napkin and pick up a fork to eat. We eat in silence for a moment, even though I can feel the tension around the table.

"Eris," Dad says, "I know we've mentioned this before. I really wish you would reconsider seeing a therapist. Just to help you get your thoughts together after what you've been through."

"I'm fine, Dad," I say. "Better than fine, actually." I feel desperate to change the subject. "You know, all the time I was away, I did not have one migraine? And still no migraine? I think I've outgrown the headaches."

He stares at me for a long moment, his smile faltering. "Well, the medication is potent. Best selling pain medication on the market."

"I haven't been taking the pills. I, uh, forgot them when I left home and I couldn't get anymore, so...so I just haven't been taking them. And no headaches."

Mother's eyes first got wide, then a stiff smile appeared on her face. "Well, that's good. That's...that's great. You must have grown out of them. I've heard of things like that happening"

"You've stopped taking your medication?" Dad set down his fork and glared at me, a scowl on his face. "You need to take that medication. Every day."

"Yeah, I know, but that was back when I was having migraines. I'm not anymore, though, so—"

"Have you taken them since you got home?"

I hesitate, unable to read the look on his face. Is this anger? Is he really angry with me for not taking unnecessary pain meds?

"I don't need them," I say. "I'm not having headaches—"

He slammed his fist on the table. His plate jumps, nearly spilling all over the tablecloth. "You need to take them, Eris. Everyday. It's non-negotiable. It's important that you take them every day. Do you understand?"

I stare at him, stunned and confused by his violent reaction. "Dad...why do I have to take them? Why do I need migraine medication when I'm not having migraines?"

Dad wipes his face angrily and Mom looks down at her plate timidly, like she's afraid Dad will attack her or something. He's not looking at Mom right now, though. He's glaring at me.

"Listen to me carefully," he says, "you will take that medication every day from this point on. Do you understand me?"

"Dad—"

"Do you understand?!"

"Of course, I understand! Just tell me why! I'm not in pain anymore. This doesn't make sense."

"Don't argue with me," he warns. "Either you take the pills, or I'll admit you to the hospital and I'll have them give it to you through an IV. It is for your own good and you will take them every morning."

"Okay," I say, putting my hands up in surrender. "Whatever you say, Dad."

"Good," he says. He goes back to eating his meal like nothing happened. I've lost my appetite, though. I push my plate away from me and stand up.

"Where are you going?" Mom asks.

"You haven't been excused from the table, young lady."

"I'm not hungry," I say as I walk away.

I got to my room and sat on my bed, too angry to think. I look over at the jar of pills on my nightstand. These stupid pills Dad wants me to take I clearly don't need. What is the big fucking deal anyway? Why would he threaten to force-feed the medication to me?

I pick up the jar and open it, viewing the purple pills for a long moment. I screw the top back on and walk across the room to stash it in my dresser drawer.

Why? Could I have some condition other than migraines that this medicine helps? But if I do, why wouldn't Dad just say something?

I grab my laptop and sit on my bed. Surely, the indications are listed on the net. I type in the medication name, Levantus Doxate, and immediately, I find a list of information on it. Where one can purchase it, information about the company, blah, blah, blah.

Starting another search, this time adding the words 'medical indications', the new results pop up quickly with a bulleted list.

- Migraine and pain relief

- Muscle Relaxer

Continuing to read, I run across a list of side effects and contraindications, stopping to make some notes.

- Nausea

- Aura and/or vertigo

- Mildly decreased magical libido (Not for mage use)

What the hell? Magical libido? And in parenthesis, not for mage use? What the hell?

I click on the company website and scroll to the side effects. The first line reads, *Not recommended for mage use as it causes mildly decreased magical libido. While most mages report a mild shift in their powers, this medication is indicated primarily for human usage.*

What about a human who has powers? I muse. Probably not indicated for me either. Mages who have taken the drug report their powers have weakened, but no one reports them gone altogether. I find a chat board with mages reporting the side effects and a few of them suggesting they use the medication to sneak into human spaces.

For every person who suggests it, there's someone immediately debunking it. The effects aren't strong enough to wipe them out entirely. Or It just feels like you're congested. You can still cast, just not very strongly.

Hmm. That's interesting. So, theoretically, by taking these meds, I shouldn't be shut down completely. And yet, I haven't been able to do any magic since I got home and I haven't taken a single pill. That's odd, too.

I keep researching, finding nothing linking the pills to my particular lack of magical ability. Maybe I'm barking up the wrong tree here. Maybe something else is blocking my magic and the pills were helping me somehow. I am somewhat of an anomaly.

Wait...what's that?

I'm on the company website when I happen to scroll past a photo of the pill. I scroll back...and there it is. A white pill with a line carved down the middle.

White. A white pill. The pills in my dresser are purple.

"Oh...no," I whisper. I get up and get the pills from my dresser, opening the jar and looking at the plain purple pills. No line. No stamp. Just round and purple.

What are these? Where did they come from? I stand there for a long time, unsure of what to make of this...

I always get these from Dad's pharmacy. Always. Even though I see the commercials for the medication. Even though I know it exists in other pharmacies. I've never gotten them anywhere but at my Dad's pharmacy.

Dear God...what are these?

I rush to my bathroom, dump the entire bottle into the bowl, and flush. As they swirl down the drain and out of sight, the hum of magic grows in volume around me. I take in a deep breath. I feel like I've been seeing the world in black and white and now it's in full color again. Was it the pills all along?

Has my migraine medicine suppressed my magic all these years? I stand in the bathroom for a long moment. Shock cools to thoughtfulness and I return to my bed to consider this revelation.

It's true. I can't deny or ignore it. As soon as those pills were away from me, the magic returned.

Has my Dad been poisoning me? No. He's been suppressing my powers.

That means he knew. But how could he know? I have no memories of ever using my powers around him or anyone else. I've never had any reason to believe I was any different than anyone else.

I have to know the answer. And there's only one way, short of asking him directly, which I am certain is not a good idea.

No, I'll take the next best option; I'll go into his study tonight after they've gone to bed. Surely, there's something there that will tell me what I need to know.

***

It's late. Or early. After midnight so officially the early hours of a new day. I am just outside the door to my father's study. All is quiet. Just as I reach for the door handle, I realize the door is slightly ajar and I freeze. It's always closed unless he's inside.

"Randall, I'm going up to bed. Are you coming soon?"

It's my mother's voice. She's in the study. They are both in the study. I slowly turn to retrace my steps and pause as I hear his response.

"You go on up. I want to finish the new batch of Levantus for Eris. I've increased the dosage. No more magic spilling out and creating issues once she's on this version."

"Are you sure?" Her voice is timid and it occurs to me that I've never heard her speak any other way to him. How could I have missed the fact that this woman is terrified of her husband?

"If she isn't having headaches, can't we just let her be herself?"

"Woman! Don't speak foolishness." His voice is as cold and angry as it was at the dinner table when he threatened me. "She can never be allowed to touch magic in any way. You know this."

"Don...Don't be angry, please Randall. I am sorry. Yes. Yes. I know. I'm being a foolish woman."

I'm stunned. Unable to process what I heard, I put it aside, realizing I couldn't be caught eavesdropping. As quietly and quickly as I can, I return to my room and gently close the door, jumping into my bed seconds before she opens the door and peeks in.

"Good night, sweety. Sleep well," she whispers before closing the door.

CHAPTER TWENTY

MAC

• • • • • • • • • • •

FOUR DAYS NOW I'VE been without Eris. Aside from the throbbing pain in my shoulder, the pain of being forcibly separated from her is nearly unbearable.

I was lucky. Damned lucky. They pulled her out of my reach so easily. We did not have a chance against the sting her father engineered. Had I not opened that portal, they'd have finished me off in broad daylight.

Missy plops a tray of steaming food on the picnic table in front of me. I see she's wearing her kutte today. I nod in thanks, and she heads back toward the temporary clubhouse Lillian is allowing the Maztecs to live in.

Soup with a grilled cheese sandwich and a glass of milk. I feel like I'm twelve years old.

"Couldn't get me a steak?" I ask.

Lillian, seated across from me with her own lunch, laughs. "I can't even get a steak. You're lucky I've got milk. You know how hard that is to come by?"

I look at the glass of white skeptically. "Cow's milk?"

"Goat," she says, "Eat up. You need your strength."

"Yes, Ma'am." I pick up the sandwich with my good hand and she smiles at me gently. "I'm glad to see you're okay. You had us worried sick."

"I guess I'm harder to kill than they thought," I say as I dip the sandwich in the soup and take a bite.

She watches me eat for a moment, then she asks, "Are you ready to talk about it?"

I shake my head. I feel like an idiot for letting Eris meet with her father. I should have talked her out of it. Or put my foot down and forbid her to go. Yeah, sure. Like I could have forbade her. She would have gone alone and wouldn't have come back. At least this way, I know what happened to her.

Lillian nods when I don't answer her. "Then let me fill you in."

The way she says it lets me know she has news to share. I did miss the biggest chunk of the past 3 days, so I'm grateful for the update.

"The cat is fully out of the bag on shifters being able to use magic," she says. "People in the park posted cell phone video of your take down, shift to wolf, being shot, and creating the portal to escape. The cabal could not shut down the video feeds fast enough.

The authority agents delivered Eris back to her family," she says. "It's been all over the news. Her father has been heralding the Authority as heroes for bringing his daughter back to him."

"Saving her from the wretched monsters in the desert," I say listlessly. "She wanted to see her father. Lillian, I knew it was a setup, but..."

Lillian frowns at me and tilts her head. "But?"

I shake my head. The words are all jumbled again. "I thought I'd have more time...more time to tell her the truth. I just didn't have enough time."

"What truth? What have you found out?"

I take a deep breath and tell Lillian my suspicions; about Eris and her connection to Magnus Circadia; about seeing the high council ring on her father's finger; about her mysterious migraine medicine and the scepter. All of it.

She doesn't interrupt. She just sits and listens until I am done.

"I didn't know how to tell her the man she thinks is her father truly is a monster who raised her for his own nefarious reasons."

We sit in silence for several minutes before she speaks. "Finding out you're the child of the most powerful mage who has ever lived...I guess you can't just tell someone that on the fly."

"No. I should have found a way, though. If I had, she wouldn't be in the hands of those monsters."

"They're monsters to us," Lillian says. "To her, they're her parents."

"You think they won't hurt her?"

She thought about it for a moment. "I don't know. They're the only family she's ever known.

It seems unlikely they will harm her, don't you think?"

"All I know is that anyone who would order the execution of an entire family probably wouldn't be above murdering their own child. Especially since she's not his biological daughter."

"What can we do? They're in the central hub. We can't go after her."

"I don't know. I hope you're right. Maybe they'll suppress her powers again and make her go back to being human."

I think about how upset Eris was to entertain the idea that she might be a mage. Maybe she is better off this way. She gets her life back. The life I pulled her out of to keep her safe. Well. Maybe she was safe all along...

"If I could wake up tomorrow a human if I could live a life without looking over my shoulder, could travel through the city without having to worry about Hunters or Authority agents, would I want that? Would you, Lillian?"

She reaches across the table and rests her hand on my good arm, giving it a gentle squeeze. "Not a possibility I've ever considered, Mac. Honestly, who can blame Eris if that's what happens? She is probably better off in her old life. She'll go on working in the GCI, maybe find a nice human to marry eventually. Have children and hope they don't inherit her magic powers."

"Yeah. I'll catch up with you later, Lil. I need to walk off this huge feast," I say. My laugh is empty, and I am sure she realizes I just want a bit of space. "I've been sitting on my ass for too long."

I returned to the main area in time for the latest news report on the net. Sure enough, Eris' father is speaking at a news conference yet again. He is among several men standing on a dais in front of a large audience where authority agents are being given awards for bravery. Randall Loving is one of the group of dignitaries being interviewed by the reporters.

"I want to thank everyone for their good wishes," he's saying. "My daughter is home safe and sound and I am eternally grateful to the Authority for their assistance."

"Holy shit." Flip sits up in his seat. He nudges Misty, who's sitting next to him. "That's him. You see that?"

They both look up at the screen. Flip points, "Look at his hand." It's the ring. The fucking High Council ring. As plain as day.

Misty puts her hand over her mouth, then she gets up and runs from the room.

"What's that about?" I ask Flip.

"I think that guy's a big deal on the High Council."

"What guy? Loving? We know. I saw the ring when he took Eris away."

"Yeah, but there's more. Misty will explain," Flip says.

Misty ran back into the room, laptop in hand. She puts it down on the coffee table and scrolls through hundreds of photos on her drive. Both Flip and I perch on the couch on either side of her, impatient for her to speak.

"OK. High Council members don't have to be a member of the Elite Corps. But a lot of them come from the corps ranks. The leaders of the High Council mostly sit back in their ivory towers and give out laws and orders. But some of them...ah, here we go."

"He's like a general or something. Misty found a photo of him—"

She pulls up a photo of five men, all standing together in battle robes, each man wearing the ring of the High Council.

"These were the original Elite Corps team. The founding members." Misty says. "They were all humans fighting in the war. They assassinated high-ranking supernatural folk in the name of the Global Cabal. They only answered to the High Council and their whole job was taking out enemies of the GC."

"Yeah," Flip adds, "she showed this to me when she found it and I told her I seen one of these guys before. Couldn't place him until now. Check it out."

Misty zooms in on the face of one of them. Dark-skinned, wire-rimmed glasses...a bit younger than he is now...but it's definitely the same man.

My mouth has gone dry. "You have got to be shitting me."

"Randall Loving," Misty says. "Human and smart as hell. During the war, he specialized in chemical warfare. Built bombs and all that. Pretty sure he had a hand in creating Magnus' scepter."

"You think so?"

She shrugged. "I couldn't tie any of the others to the use of alchemy. He would have the knowledge to make something powerful enough to weaken one's ability to use magic."

I go silent, thinking of all the implications, but mainly considering what this means for Eris.

Someone had to keep her power concealed and he would be the one who could do it, just like he tried to weaken Magnus. Crafty son of a bitch.

"He sounds like a pretty dangerous dude," says Flip, "but is he the kind of guy who would hurt his own daughter?"

"I don't know," I say, my shoulder aching. "But I don't think we should wait to find out. We need to find a way to get to her. To warn her."

"Good luck with that," Misty says. "The second we step foot in the central hub, we'll be arrested."

"Doesn't matter. We have to figure out a way to get to her. If he's been suppressing her power all this time, what happens if he finds out that she can do magic? He might hurt her just to keep her docile. We can't let that happen."

We all look at each other for a long moment, the reality of what lies before us coming crystal clear.

"Well," Flip says, "We've staged a big break-in before. I guess we can do it again. Count me in."

"Me, too," says Misty.

"And me," Lillian says from across the room. She downs the rest of the drink she's having and walks over to us. She'd been listening to us the whole time. "Anything I can do to help, I'm at your disposal."

"Good," I say. "It won't be easy. But when is anything ever easy for this club?"

Flip slaps his hands together. "Let's do it. I've been itching to get my hands on one of those rat bastards."

And so it's on.

CHAPTER
TWENTY-ONE

Eris

• • • • • • • • • •

A S THE REFRESHING WAVES of water from
the shower wash over me, I feel like my
mind has been washed clean as well. Sleep did not
come after Mom left my door. I've looked at this
from every direction I can. The facts are clear,
although pieces are still missing.

Fact number one: The reason the Levantus
Doxate pills on the company website do not look
like the ones I take is because Dad has been
manufacturing a version of the drug just for me.

Now I understand why, the minute he found out I stopped taking the purple pills, the air in the room changed. In fact, he was fucking pissed last night.

I get dressed, putting on a simple T-shirt and jeans and I sit on my bed to think about fact number two: my powers. It's weird I have them in the first place and is a separate fact I'll have to circle back to. But it is a fact magic went dead for me until I flushed the pills. Ever since I can hear the air moving again. I can feel the energy of the magic within me. Even though I did not take any, just being in the same room closed down my ability to touch the arcane.

God, my head is pounding from almost no sleep and a heavy cloud of paranoia is hanging over me. I need answers. I still think I should snoop through Dad's things. It may not be the best choice, but at least it's doing something, and I can't think of any better way to learn the truth.

I'll have to wait until he goes to work today.

"Eris?" I hear from beyond my bedroom door. It's Mom calling me from the bottom of the stairs. "Breakfast!"

I'm not hungry. I've got a good mind to not come down at all. I guess if I did that, though, they'd probably come up here instead to make sure I'm all right. I don't trust them anymore.

As I come down the stairs and into the hallway leading to the kitchen, I can see the table bathed in morning sunlight from the bay window. Dad is already sitting with his plate of toast and eggs in front of him. He's drinking coffee and scrolling through the news posts on the net on his tablet. Mom is deeper in the kitchen speaking softly to him.

Just another morning. I feel like I'm a kid again coming down these stairs.

"Morning," I say as I walk into the room. Mom's at the kitchen counter and as soon as I walk in, she smiles at me, bringing me my plate.

"Morning, Dumpling," she says. "Did you sleep well?"

"Yeah," I lie. "Slept like a baby." I look over at Dad, who hasn't even looked up from his tablet. He's still pissed at me, I guess. I'd better make nice. "I've been thinking about it and...I think maybe you guys are right. I should see a therapist."

They both look at me. My mom looks over at Dad eagerly. He sets down his tablet. "Good," he says. "You've been through a great deal of trauma. It can only help you in the end."

I nod and pick up my fork, poking at my eggs, but I don't really respond to that. He smiles at me and I think of how strange it looks this morning. I used to look forward to seeing that smile. It used to mean that everything was okay.

"So," he says, "you'll go back to taking your medication, then?"

"Yeah, sure," I lie again. Then an idea pops into my head and I add, "Speaking of which, I was thinking about it and, you know, I can get a discount at the pharmacy across the street from work because I work for GCI. I could save money and get it from there from now on instead of going all the way to this side of town to get it."

Both their faces change, but just slightly. Mom looks down at her plate and eats a bite of eggs. Dad's still smiling, though his eyes look darker somehow. "A discount," he chuckles. "You want a discount for a medication you don't even pay for? That doesn't make any sense."

"It's no big deal," I say. I can feel my hands start to get sweaty as the feeling of impending danger comes over me. "I looked it up. Turns out it's not that expensive. I mean, you guys are going through so much just to take care of me, I don't want to be a burden. This way, it's one less thing you've got to do every month."

His smile slides away and he takes a drink of his coffee before speaking. "What are you trying to pull?"

Shit. I keep my cool, chuckling. "Sorry?"

"I said, what are you trying to pull, Eris?" he repeats, raising his voice. "I thought I was clear with you last night. Taking your medication is non-negotiable."

"Who said anything about not taking it? I'll still be taking it."

"How will we know that? You say you want to go to another pharmacy and pay for it rather than get it from me because it's more convenient. Why don't you cut the bullshit? I'm not a complete fool."

"Randall!" Mom objects, "Please stop this!"

"Why are you hell-bent on me taking a medication I don't need, Dad?" I say, ignoring my mother. "I haven't had a migraine in a week, without the medication. Is there some other reason I should take the pills?"

We stare at each other across the table but I'm not backing down. This is his chance to clear it all up for me. He can get rid of my paranoia by just telling me what the big fucking deal is.

"That's enough. Both of you." Mom says. "This fighting is ridiculous, and I will not have it in my house. You two have to come to an understanding about this."

"There's no disagreement to resolve," Dad says as he gets up from the table. "Eris, you will take your medication, or we will have it forcibly administered to you. It's as simple as that."

Without another word, he walks out of the kitchen. Mom sighs and a few seconds later, we hear the front door slam shut. "Why are you making this so difficult?" she asks me. "There's no harm to you in taking the medication. It's no different than you've done since you were ten years old."

"Mom. I don't understand why I have to keep taking medication if it's clear that I don't need it. Why is that a problem?"

She opens her mouth to speak, then stops herself, deciding against whatever thought has just surfaced. "It's not a problem," she says, finally. "Listen, I realize this is just a byproduct from your kidnapping, so...so, we'll discuss it further after you start working it all out in therapy."

I don't know what to make of that. She clears hers and my father's plates and takes them to the sink to wash them. "It'll all be fine," she says. "You'll see."

I watch her wash the dishes as I pick through my breakfast. It most certainly will not be fine. It may never be fine again...

***

It's an hour later and Mom just left for work. I'm sitting on the top of the stairs, listening for her car to pull out of the driveway. Once it does, I start down the stairs to Dad's study.

I get to the door of Dad's study, and I grab the knob. The door doesn't budge. Locked? Are you serious right now? It's never locked. Why should it be? There's nothing but books in there.

I think for a moment. I could let this go now. Just give in to my parents and go to therapy and take meds I don't need.

But then the magic might stop again and...and I don't want it to stop. It's scary as shit, I'll admit, but I can't deny it's been a boon to know I have all this power at my fingertips...

Right. I have all this power at my fingertips. Hmm.

I close my eyes and listen to the swirling air around me, then I take in a breath and let it fill me. My body vibrates, the energy moving through all the way to my fingers.

Locked doors. I touch the doorknob and I think only one word. UNLOCK.

I hear the door click, the knob sliding away from my fingers. "Ha!" I yelp, then cover my mouth as if someone might hear me. Locked doors are no longer a problem for this girl.

Inside, I'm surrounded by the smell of wood and book paper. My Dad's study and all its trappings are all so familiar to me. The wall of bookshelves, the big oak desk. The whole room smells faintly of him; his cologne and those god-awful cigarettes he likes. I walk over to his desk where there's an ancient-looking glass dish filled with ashes, bits of paper, and burnt tobacco.

I feel nostalgia for him...for this. I remember being a kid and coming in here to read the books on the shelves while he typed up reports on his computer. There's much here I associate with good memories.

I sit in his chair and sigh, second-guessing my determination. My father can't be some evil villain. He's my Dad. I look at the papers neatly piled on the blotter. Reports and lists of drug interactions. In another pile, studies about medication usage.

I lean back as I look around and notice something. Small, insignificant, barely even noticeable. It's a dull, silver circle under the desktop. I rub my finger over it and find it's got a soft, movable part in the center. A button! I press it.

Behind me, there's a mechanical sliding noise. I turn to see the bookshelf moving slowly to one side, revealing a room. I can't make out anything but shapes. The light from the study helps me with that.

Well. This is something new. I get up and walk into the room, feeling around one of the walls for a light switch. I find one and flick it on.

There's one wall full of old, dusty books on one side of the room and on the other a worktable. I walk close to the work table and see pieces of plants, herbs, and bits of purple flowers. There are tools here as well. Tiny pairing knives and a crucible. Hanging above the table is a drying rack with bunches of purple flowers dangling from the baskets.

As I stand here, I feel woozy. The smell of the flowers is making my head spin.

When I step away and go to the books, my head clears. There's one book in particular that's sticking out from its place on the shelf as if it were put back in a hurry, or maybe stuck out so as not to get lost in the shuffle with the other books.

The books have strange writing on them or are titled oddly. There's one called Herbs and Potions. Another is called Healing Medicinals. The book that's sticking out has written on it, *Rare Herbs and Their Uses.*

I take it out and open it. It's marked and highlighted to death with dogeared pages and bits of writing in the margins. This has been heavily studied. My eyes are drawn to a woodcutting, the spitting image of the purple flowers hanging in the drying racks behind me. It's labeled, Orudis Root. I read through the first paragraph and my stomach tightens as soon as I see it.

...commonly used for pain relief among humans, but fresh sprigs have been known to be useful for temporary magic suppression.

It's true. Oh, my God.

"What are you doing in here?"

I drop the book at the sound of the voice and whirl around. My father is standing at the room's entrance, blocking out the light from the study.

CHAPTER TWENTY-TWO

MAC

• • • ● • ● • ● • • •

I FIND IT IRONIC the one clue I had to my parent's deaths is also going to get us through these gates.

Last night, Flip, Misty, Lillian, and I got busy making a plan to get Eris. Flip and Misty did their magic on the computer, finding the Loving home address within a few hours. Lillian and I gathered a few of her people to work on getting us a van and by the time the sun was rising, we had a destination, a small team, and a vehicle to get beyond the gates leading into the central hub.

Mages or any magical being can be detected within the confines of the hub. I remembered what Lillian said about Orudis Root being used to mask magic by some mages and I thought about the scepter and how every time I was near it, my powers shorted out. We didn't have any Orudis Root, but I'm willing to bet having it on me while we sneak into the hub will hide us.

It's a wild bet. This thing is old, which is probably why it never stopped my powers entirely. But even if we can get their sensors to come back haywire, that might be enough to fool the authorities at the gates.

Misty gets to drive, being that she's the least wanted out of all of us in this van. She had the brilliant idea to choose a pretty blue dress and is even wearing make-up. Her short curls are fluffed up so that they fall in her face when she moves her head. She looks good. Let's hope she looks good enough to fool these guys.

"Showtime," she says as we pull up to the gate. In the back of the van, Flip, Lillian, and two of her best bear shifters are sitting with me, waiting in silence.

"Hi, there," Misty says in a voice that's too high. "It's a nice day, isn't it?"

I hear the checkpoint guy clear his throat. "Yes, it is. Where you headed?"

"Middle Ring," she says. "I'm an interior decorator."

There's a pause and my heart pounds in my chest. "Oh, yeah," he says. "All by your lonesome?"

"I've got a crew coming later," she says. "I'm just driving the van in so that they can come in their own cars. We're burning daylight, you know? I want to at least have the carpet laid before noon."

"I hear that." This guard sounds friendly. He's buying Misty's bullshit. "As pretty as you are, I'm sure you know your way around decorating a house."

I hear Flip stifle a laugh and I throw him a look of warning. He pulls his knees to his chest and buries his head.

"I most certainly do. What time do you get off work, cowboy?"

I roll my eyes. We do not have time for this.

"Not until late. Double shift."

"Oh, yeah? Well, maybe I'll see you on my way out, huh?"

"Yeah...yeah, maybe you will."

There's another pause and I feel a slight bit of panic as I realize they're probably running a scan. "Hmm," I hear the guard say. "Looks like you maybe got magic residue going on. You been through any mage districts lately?"

"I don't think so—Oh, wait. I had to drive through Madentown. Maybe that's what you're picking up?"

"Probably. Anyway, have a good day. You're free to pass."

"Bye-bye." And the van is moving again. Thank the heavens.

"'As pretty as you are, I'm sure you know your way around decorating a house,'" Flip mocks with a twangy accent. "God, that guy's got no game."

"No kidding," Misty says with a laugh. "I had to throw him a bone. I felt bad for him."

"Focus, please," I say. I'm in no mood for jokes. "Can we just get there so we can get Eris and get back before anybody notices us?"

"Relax," says Misty. "We're good. The hard part is over."

I just shake my head uselessly. Lillian nudges me. "Relax," she says. "It's all going according to plan. We passed the first hurdle."

I nod, letting her reassurance take me. Think positive...just think positive.

***

There aren't any signs anyone's here. I'm leaning between the seats, looking out of the front windshield to study the scene. The house had no cars in the driveway and the windows all had the shades drawn. "Doesn't look good."

"They don't look home," Misty observes, and I see Flip jeer.

"No shit. What do we do if they're not home?"

I think for a second. I guess it's possible Eris went back to work. It's nearing the middle of the morning, after all. There might not be anything here to see.

"Don't tell me we did all this for nothing," Misty crossed her arms in a huff.

"We still have to check," I decide. "Just because it looks like no one's home doesn't mean it's true. We'll do a quick look around the house. If she's not there, then we'll decide what comes next. Come on."

We get out of the truck and walk to the house, leaving the scepter behind in the truck. I'm going to need as much magic as I can get if we run into trouble out here. I'm looking around for security devices. There don't appear to be any. This looks like a normal house in the Middle Ring. I'm half expecting there to be a picket fence in the front yard.

Flip steps forward and taps the doorknob, unlocking it with his magic. "Presto," he says.

I look around at the other houses cautiously. "Let's go," I say. "Quickly."

We're inside and, what can I say? This is a house. A small foyer and a hallway with a staircase leading up to the second floor. A living room to the left and a dining room to the right. I look down the hall and see a kitchen...maybe a den or a study or something around the corner behind the stairs. As I step all the way in, I listen for any sign of life in the house.

"Doesn't look like anybody's here," says Lillian. "What do you want to do?"

"Lil, take your guys and search upstairs. Flip and Misty, fan out. Help me check downstairs.

Flip went into the dining room and Misty went in the other direction to the living room. I walk straight down the hall towards the kitchen. I lean into the well-lit area and see no one's there, then

I turn down the hallway and find a room just off the corridor. The door's ajar, so I go in.

It's a study. Lots of bookshelves and an old Persian rug. There is an oak desk and an oddly placed door to a room behind the desk. As I walk towards it, I realize that I'm looking at the open door of a secret room. I look at the bookshelf moved to one side. Clearly, it's what was hiding the room originally.

The room looks like an alchemy room. Immediately, I feel my magic weakening. Above the workbench is a row of purple flowers. Orudis Root, no doubt.

This is where he did it. This is where Randall Loving made the pills to suppress Eris' powers. But if this door is open, where's Randall? More importantly, where's Eris?

"Hey, boss." I turn to see Misty at the door of the study. She pauses, her eyes looking over the hidden room. "Holy shit. Is this what I think it is?"

"If you think it's a secret alchemy room, then yes. What's up?"

She looks at me and says, "So, Flip and I found the basement. You'll never guess what's down there."

"Don't have time to guess, Misty."

"Right, right." She clears her throat. "We think there's a door hidden in one of the walls. Maybe it's another hidden room."

I sigh as I take another look around this room. "A house with a bunch of hidden secrets. That can't be good."

"It's not great," she chimes in.

"All right. Let's go," I say, following her back out in the hall. As soon as we're at the stairs, Lillian's standing on the landing.

"Nobody's up here," she calls down.

"Stay on the first floor and keep watch," I tell them. "We maybe found something in the basement."

"You sure you don't want us to come with?"

I shake my head. "We don't want to get jumped if anybody comes home unexpectedly."

"Roger that."

Misty leads me through the kitchen and to a door on the far side of the room. We open it and I go down first, diving into the dim light of what looks like an oddly organized basement. I can't see a lot, but I can make out the shapes of storage boxes on shelves lined up along the cement wall. There are plastic containers all stacked up in corners. There are windows above us that let in enough light for us to see where we're going, but it's a pretty dark and dank basement all around.

I see Flip standing by one of the walls, pressing his hands against it while he leans in as if he's listening to something.

"Flip—"

"Shh," he says quickly. I look over at Misty, who just shrugs. After a few more moments, Flip slides his hand up to the molding and presses it with his fingers. The wall slowly slides to one side, revealing a hallway. We stand there for a moment while stale air rushes out to meet us.

"I guess this isn't just an ordinary house," says Flip.

"It most certainly is not," I answer.

"Who has a tunnel in their basement?" Misty muses. "This just jumped up a level in creepiness."

I step forward, peering into the darkness. I can't see too far down it. I lift my hand, creating a light from my fingertips and the walls illuminate, revealing gray slate on all sides. There aren't any cobwebs or dirt. It's weirdly and immaculately clean.

"You don't suppose there's anybody down there...do you?" Flip says.

"Come on," I tell both him and Misty. "There's only one way to find out."

We start down the hallway and into the darkness.

CHAPTER TWENTY-THREE

ERIS

• • • • • • • • • • •

"**O**w!" My father yanks the rope tight around my wrists, binding them tightly in front of me.

"Sorry," he says. "I can't have you getting loose."

When he found me in his secret room, he didn't even wait for an explanation for my presence. He grabbed me by the back of my neck and dragged me through the house, down to the basement, and into a tunnel. A fucking tunnel! I grew up in this house. I never knew there was a tunnel! Why is there a fucking tunnel?

The tunnel led to a bunker that I also didn't know anything about. I'm looking up and around at shelves of jars with oddly colored powders and liquids in them. He's got medieval-looking tools and knives hanging from hooks on walls and old dusty books on a table off to the side.

What is this place? I start to shake as he stands up and sighs, looking down at me and shaking his head.

"I was hoping it would not come to this," he says. "All these years keeping you safe. I hoped we'd never be here."

"Dad?" I say and I can hear the fear in my own voice. "Why...why are you doing this?"

He sighs, looking at me the way he does when he's disappointed in me. He grabs a chair and pulls it in front of me. Then he sits down, leaning with his elbows on his knees as he speaks.

This reminds me of the times when I was young and he would 'have a talk' with me. Like the time I accidentally broke a window while playing stickball with my friends. Or the time I snuck a boy into my room. This is his 'we need to have a serious talk about your behavior' stance. It's insane it's happening now in this room with my hands bound.

"I might as well tell you the truth, I guess," he says. "I didn't think I'd ever have to. You were doing so well."

He pauses and looks away from me, his eyebrows turned up and his mouth in a deep-set frown. "Plans of mice and men, I guess."

"Dad." My voice is breaking, and I feel a sob coming on. I swallow, doing my best to keep the tears away. As terrifying as this is, I can't lose it. Not now. "Why are you doing this to me? I don't understand."

He looks over at me, his dark eyes settling on my face. He removes his glasses and folds them, putting them in his shirt pocket. "It's time you knew the truth, my darling. As much as your mother and I have cared for you and loved you as our own...the fact is that you're not my daughter."

I didn't hear him right. He didn't just say what I think he did. Or I'm misunderstanding him. "Wh-what?"

He takes a deep breath. He looks like he's lifting a great weight off his shoulders. "I guess if I'm going to explain what that means, I'll have to tell you everything else, won't I? Eris, when you were born, the war was going our way thanks to Magnus Circadia. He was single-handedly winning the war for us. You've read all the books on him, right? Seen all the documentaries. I always thought it was interesting you were drawn to the history of Circadia and how our nation was formed."

He smiles and I glimpse the man I know as my father shine through. It only lasts for a moment, though.

"They're all lies," he says coldly, the smile dissolving. "Every single reference. The only part they got right is that he was the most powerful mage who ever lived."

He looks away from me, off to someplace in the past. "Oh, darling, you should have seen him fight. He moved like he could see the blows before they were coming. His magic, he was precise in his aim. He could pluck the eye off a shifter from more than a hundred yards. It was a glory to see him in battle. He was our prize. The one great hope for the Cabal."

I swallow hard, my mouth is as dry as the desert. "You...you were never in the war, Dad. You said because of your eyesight, you couldn't join the ranks of the Cabal in any capacity—"

"There's nothing wrong with my eyes, darling," he says simply.

I see the edges of his glasses in his shirt pocket and my heart sinks further. He always wore them. Always. For as long as I can remember, he's talked about his poor eyesight, he...he...

"But humans don't..." I can't get it out. I try again. "They didn't fight in the war. We didn't fight..." The tears are coming. They burn my eyes as they roll down my cheeks. He leans forward and wipes them away with his thumb.

"You see, during the war, we were very pleased with the rise of Magnus Circadia. He was commanding armies and bringing us victory after victory. But the High Council, in all their wisdom, saw he would turn that great strength against us, and we would have no defense. We feared when the war was done, he would fight the Cabal next. It was decided he needed to be controlled. Contained."

He sits back in his chair, looking at me with a smile on his face. "That's when I got the call. I was a professor at the local university and word had gotten out that I knew a great deal about alchemy and herbal work. The High Council asked me to create a device to bind his magic, prevent him from using magic. They promised if I did that, then I would earn a spot among the most elite of the high council members. I would become one of an exclusive, highly secret society. All I had to do was hobble the great Magnus Circadia.'

"The first attempt worked well. I created a scepter made from silver and infused it with a special herb I knew could shackle mages and their magic without ever laying a hand on them. He took the gift eagerly and almost immediately found his powers weakened." He chuckles to himself. "It was genius. Over a short period of time, however, not only did his powers return, but they got stronger. Much stronger than we'd anticipated. He was laying waste to entire armies with a wave of his hand. The war was won in a matter of days."

He sighs and he gets up from the chair and walks over to the worktable. "As soon as the treaty was signed, the order of execution was made and the team I led was assigned to carry out the executions."

I don't want to hear anymore. I wish I could put my hands to my ears. "What did you do?" I whisper. He's looking at the one book on the table, opening it, then slowly turning its pages.

"He had to die," he replies softly. "More importantly we had to ensure no one could follow in his footsteps, not if we were going to know peace. No mage could ever be that powerful again.

It was too dangerous. The threat to the Cabal was untenable."

He's stopped turning the pages. His finger is pressed on one of the pages as he gazes down at it, his bottom lip trembling.

"We went to the Circadia home one night and covered the floors and the halls with the Orudis plant. Hung it from the walls, twisted it around their staircase railing...purple petals everywhere. We spread it all over their home and we waited until dawn. We found the children unconscious and one by one we slit each of their throats. Magnus and Loris his wife fought us but were too weakened by the orudis and they died trying to flee from their bedroom."

I start to sob, closing my eyes as if I can block out the mental image of my father taking a blade to the necks of an entire family. How...how could he?

"We did not find Alura, the youngest. I sent the others away and set the explosives to destroy the house and all evidence of the Circadia family. I waited because I like explosions.

It was a magnificent blast. Destroyed everything. Nearly. When the dust cleared and the fire died down, I was amazed to see a king-sized bed sitting completely intact on top of the debris and untouched by the blast or the fires still burning in pockets. He pauses again, his hand sliding off the book. "I made my way to the bed and looked down at this perfect little girl, round cheeks and beautiful dark eyes and all that curly hair. Your mother and I had been trying for a child for years with no luck. And as cruel as you might think me to be, I didn't have it in me to end the life of a toddler barely able to walk.

I feel like I'm going to throw up. I can't believe what he's saying right now. I can't...I can't believe it...

He pushes the book over to me. "I did the only thing a reasonable person would do in that situation. I picked you up and brought you home." He pointed to the page in the book. It's a photo album, and there I am as an infant. It's a photo I've never seen before. Professionally done. I'm in a white dress and bonnet, looking at the camera with cherubic innocence...and sitting on the lap of the great Magnus Circadia.

Under the photo, the caption is written, Magnus Circadia, with daughter, Alura Eris Circadia.

"So, you see," he says, "that's what the pills are for. We decided to raise you as a human. To give you every opportunity and advantage in this world. But we knew the day would come when you would start to show signs of being a mage. Your mother and I worried so about when that fateful day would come. I'd already become an expert working with Orudis root. The scepter was only the beginning. I figured twelve or so years would be more than enough time to perfect a pill that would keep your powers from manifesting."

Don't you see? We did the most loving thing parents could do. We made you human."

Mac was right. I didn't start this life as a human. I am...I've always been a mage. I can taste the bile on the back of my throat, my horror threatening to come up in the form of vomit. "You...you stole my life," I whimper, hot tears rolling down my face. "Everything that I might've been...you took it from me."

"I gave you your life, Eris." He leans in as he says it, his voice raised. "You would have died along with the rest of your wretched family if not for me. I gave you a life worthy of living in this new world we were creating." He takes hold of my hands. I want to recoil from him. I loathe his touch.

"Humans are the dominant life form on this planet and always will be," he says. "What better position for you to be in? You are among the ruling class, Eris and that is because of me. Because of what I did for you."

He touches my face and I flinch from his touch. "Oh, Eris, my darling...I did this because I love you. I have loved you from the moment I found you. And I have only ever wanted the best for you."

I stiffen and swallow, forcing back the tears and the terror. "What happens now?" I ask him. "You can't...you can't get away with this. It's...it's at best illegal. At worst..." I can't even finish the sentence.

He nods sagely. "Well, then...that depends on you, doesn't it? If I let you go, you could turn me in...but like it or not, your mother and I are the only parents you've ever known. Are you willing to send your own parents to prison, Eris?"

I'm at a complete loss, my mind desperately trying to process this horror that's in front of me. A smile returns to his face. "Of course not," he whispers. "You're not the kind of woman who would hurt her own family. How about I propose an alternative?"

He took the book from my hands, walking it back over to the worktable. "You can go back to your old life," he says. "You'll have to take your medication daily and stay with us for a while longer just to make sure you're adjusting well to the new dosage. In no time, you'll be back to your home, your job with the GCI, and the safety and comfort you've been accustomed to. It's a cold world outside of the central hub, Eris. It's a different world when life becomes all about survival.

I believe you've had a taste of this truth in the past week. As an ordinary mage, you will suffer in ways you never thought possible. Out there, you'll be no one. Legally designated as a second-class citizen with no rights. Is that what you really want for yourself?"

He turns to me, a soft smile on his face to show me his benevolence. "Stay with me. Everything will be back the way it was before you were taken. This nightmare will finally be over."

He looks like the man I've seen as my father my entire life. It's this man who taught me how to ride a bike and read bedtime stories to me at night, who protected me from the imaginary monsters in my closet. And as horrified and betrayed as I feel, there is an appeal to what he's suggesting. My life was not an unhappy one before Mac and the club interrupted everything. I was making good money at a good job where I was respected and praised. It was the kind of life people envied.

But returning to it without magic? It would be like going back to a slumber I didn't know I was under. I'd lose the feeling of magic coursing through my veins. I'd lose the beauty of the starry sky in the desert at night. I did not know what I was missing and now that I do, how can I live without it?

More than all of that, though...I'd lose Mac. I am certain he survived the attack in the park. The portal he created was the last thing I saw before they bundled me into a car and whisked me away. I know he's alive. The scar on my shoulder aches the moment I think of him.

Forever...

"No," I say to him. "I can't come back. You don't know what you are asking me to give up."

His face becomes a stone mask and he turns away from me moving to the knives hanging on the wall. "I was so hoping you would cooperate," he says as he takes the largest knife from the hook. "I never wanted this day to come."

He turns around, the long blade in his hand. Terror seizes me. In some maddening way, I realize it makes sense that he would turn to killing me. I wasn't the human child he wanted, and I never would be.

He takes a step towards me, and I hear something inexplicable. The knob on the steel door jiggles and he turns to it, a look of surprise on his face. No one's supposed to be down here.

"Help!" I scream. "Help me! I'm being held hostage."

He steps forward and smacks me with the hilt of the knife. "Shut up!" he hisses.

Sharp pain shoots through me and I feel a change inside; it's like a door's been opened deep inside of me. In a heartbeat, the swirling magic around me builds and grows until I feel like I'm floating on the crest of a rushing wave. It's so strange...I could barely feel my magic at all a minute ago.

There's pounding on the steel door, but it sounds like it's a million miles away.

I lift my hands, pushing the force of the magic out to my fingertips and at the knife. It flies from my father's hands and across the room.

He's surprised but not deterred. The next thing I feel is his boot against my chest as he kicks me backward.

Me and the chair fall back with a clatter. I've lost my breath, but I'm not out just yet. I'm on my side, facing the door. *OPEN* I think.

The click of the unlocking door is audible an instant before the click of a gun's hammer being pulled back.

My father has replaced the knife with a gun trained on my head.

CHAPTER TWENTY-FOUR

MAC

• • • • • • • • • •

THE TUNNEL GOES ON forever, down a slant, so we're moving deeper underground. The air's getting cooler as we go. So much so that Misty complains about it. I glance back to see her rubbing bare arms.

"Should have worn your kutte," I say and she flips me off.

"You gonna take that, boss?" Flip jokes.

"She'll get hers when we get back," I say. I turn to face the front again and I see something glinting off the light from my fingertips. I stop and Flip and Misty stop with me.

"A door," says Flip. "All this for one room?"

"Might be more than that," I say. "A door could lead to more hallways."

"F-fantastic," Misty shivers.

We get to the door and Flip steps in front of me. "Step aside," he says. Touches the knob and it doesn't budge. He tilts his head and tries it again, but nothing happens.

"Thought you had the whole picking lock trick handled?" I say.

Flip shrugs. "Thought I did. Never ran into this before."

"It's probably not even locked," says Misty, pushing past us to the door. "Move."

She jiggles the handle, but the door remains in place. "Dammit." She's about to say something else, probably some smart-ass comment, but we hear yelling from somewhere beyond the steel barrier.

It's Eris. Yelling for help. Oh, fuck. I immediately try the knob again. When that doesn't work, I turn to Flip and Misty. "Stand back."

I drive my good shoulder into the steel, trying to force it open, but nothing happens. I step back and do it again, harder. Still nothing. I can hear shuffling somewhere beyond the door. Shit, shit, shit...

"Let me try again," says Flip.

"Maybe we can take the doorknob off," says Misty.

I step away from the door. I could try to portal. It's risky as fuck. Besides the fact that I'm noticeably weaker in this place, I could end up in a wall or a bookshelf if I miscalculate the distance. Misty and Flip must see me debating it because Flip touches my arm.

"Don't do it," he says. "It's too risky."

"We have to get in there. If I don't portal in--"

A loud click echoes around us. We all turn to the door and see it open slightly...we also hear a male voice growl, "That was a mistake."

I don't take the time to think. I push open the door. As soon as I'm in the room, I see Eris' father standing over her, a gun trained on her. She's on the floor, a chair under her, her hands bound. She sees me and a raspy yell comes at me, "Mac! Look out!"

Her father turns the gun on me. "Ah-ah," he says. "The bullets might not be silver, but I'll bet they'll still hurt like a sonofabitch."

Flip and Misty are behind me. I put my hands out to them, shielding them as best as I can. We're at a stand-off, staring each other down.

"You whole, Eris?" I say to her without looking at her.

"Yes," she says. Her voice is breathy and strained. On the floor, tied up...the wind has probably been knocked out of her.

"Let her go," I say to her father.

"I don't think so," he says. "You forget where you are, trash. You've broken into my home in the Middle Ring of the Central hub. I can have the Authority here in minutes."

I glance around the room. "It might be interesting if you did. You'd have to explain all this to them."

"I wouldn't have to explain anything. I am a well-respected man in this community. You do any harm to me and you'll never make it out of here alive."

He's not entirely wrong. If the Authority is called, no matter what, we'll have to fight and I'm not exactly at my best right now. My injured shoulder and weakened state have put me at a disadvantage even against him. Bastard probably lined the walls with Orudis Root to keep people like me at bay.

"Wait," he says suddenly, cocking his head to one side as he looks at me. "You look familiar. Where have I seen you before?"

"You don't know me, friend," I growl, fangs coming out to menace him.

"I'm certain I do. I never forget a face." His eyebrows raise suddenly and his face splits into a smile. "Did you have a brother?"

My insides twist. Sonofabitch.

"Yes...yes, you did," he goes on without waiting for me to answer. "Younger, I think, with an unfortunate name."

"His name was Obispo."

He snaps his fingers. "Obispo. Right! Santiago and Obispo Maquire. Your parents were Elena and Connor." He laughs. I don't see what's so fucking funny, but knowing my parents seems like the greatest joke he's ever heard.

"I can't believe this is happening," he says, glancing down at Eris. "What twist of fate would bring you to my doorstep of all places." He shakes his head, his eyes running across the kutte I'm wearing. Then his smile disappears as full recognition comes to him.

"Oh, my," he says softly. He looks back at Eris, then back to me. "You're the one who took her away from me. Interesting..."

"That's interesting to you?"

He nods. "You snuck into the central hub, broke into my house, and for what? For her? Why would you do something so foolish?"

"Thought that was obvious."

"It's not," he says sharply. "You're a shifter. There's absolutely no gain in this for you, even if she's aligned herself with you. There's no money to be found in rescuing her. In fact, you might've gotten a reward for her safe return instead. And yet, you are here to take her away. This is a high-risk, low-reward mission you're on right now, friend."

Everything in me is twisting around like it's caught in a vice. It's all come together now. Full circle and staring me in the face. The human who created Magnus' scepter, who perfected Orudis root enough to poison Eris...the man who just happens to know who my family was.

"Ah, well. You and your brother didn't exactly strike me as intelligent when you were children. I hear the two of you joined the service—"

"How do you know him?" It was Misty who asked it. I wish she hadn't. Randall Loving looks at me, a smile tickling the corners of his mouth.

"He's the man I've been looking for all this time," I say to her. "Not a mage. A human. And he killed my family."

"The irony that we should meet like this is so incredibly sweet," he says. "I'll bet you imagined it going in a totally different way, didn't you? And now you're here looking to rescue..."

I see it click in real time on his face. The smile disappears as he looks back down at Eris. "Dear God," he whispers. "The two of you...of course. What other force would bring a shifter behind enemy lines but love?"

He stares at me for a long moment, then turns the gun back on Eris. I take a step towards him and he edges towards her, stopping me in my tracks. "Your mother could barely move when I took her life," he says. "The scepter was a few years old by that time, but it still had a nice punch to it. When I walked into your home, she was lying on the living room floor. Your father tried to stop me...shifted into a wolf to try and tear my throat out. I shot him between the eyes with silver before he could get across the room."

I grind my teeth, a low snarl coming up from somewhere dark inside me. I want nothing more than to rip him to pieces.

"But your mother," he went on, "she was so weak and so fragile...and so beautiful. I wasn't told how beautiful she was before coming there. When I put my boot on her skull...it was like crushing a rose."

"You bastard," I growled. "You sick piece of shit."

The sinister grin on his face broadened. "You probably want your revenge," he says, "You can try to take it if you want. After she's dead, I will rip out your heart."

He pulls the trigger. The explosive pop of the gun bounces off the steel walls, temporarily deafening us all. I roar in anger at him, ready to kill him where he stood...but everything stops.

I'm frozen and so is he. The bullet from the gun hangs in the air between him and Eris. I look down with my eyes to see that the binds that were around Eris' wrists have fallen away. She lies on the floor with her hands up, beads of sweat breaking out on her forehead.

Of course. They couldn't hold her father with the Orudis Root. I guess they can't hold her either. It's taking a lot of effort, however. I can see her hands are shaking violently. She might let go any second.

She moves one shaky hand toward me and suddenly I can move again. The first thing I do is walk to the bullet and pull it out of its place in space. Then I disarm Randall. I toss both the bullet and the gun across the room, then I turn to the sonofabitch and grab him by the throat.

Eris releases him and he grabs my hands, struggling to get free of my grip. I lift him up off his feet. He gasps and struggles, kicking his legs towards me and clawing at my arm.

"You stole my life," I growled at him, my fangs out and my claws digging into his skin. "And you stole her life. Now I take yours."

I squeeze my hands around his neck and he gags, gasping for air. I let the wolf come out, strengthening my grip on him until I feel the satisfying snaps of the bones in his neck. His eyes bulge as his mouth opens in a silent scream...

And then he stops struggling. He goes limp in my hand. I let him fall to the floor.

Eris is on her feet. She walks over to stand over the man she called father her entire life. She slides her hand into mine and I realize she is sobbing. I pull her into my arms and hold her close. She lets loose, wailing into my chest. I let her cry. I don't blame her. The sound she makes is the same as the one I made the day that Biz and I found the broken bodies of our parents. She needs this grief.

I let it go until it dies down into sniffles...Then I take her face into my hands.

"We've gotta go," I say to her. "People are going to look for him and when they find him, they'll be looking for us, too." I pause before I say it. I don't want to say it, but she has to know that she has a choice.

"Flip, Misty, and me, we're already outlaws. You don't have to become one, too."

"What are you saying? You think I should stay here?"

"I'm saying...I'm saying you have a choice, Princess. You have a good life as a human. You...you don't have to give it all up."

She tilts her head at me and to my surprise, her face breaks into a smile. "What is with the men in my life wanting me to go back to nothing when I've got everything I need right in front of me?"

"Eris...I need you to be with me because you want to and not because you think you have to. My life isn't an easy one. I want you to make the right choice."

She stands on her tiptoes and kisses me. The feel of her lips are soft and pure on mine. "I know I have a choice," she says when our lips part. "I'm choosing you."

"Hey, not to ruin the moment," says Flip, "but we should probably not stick around for too much longer." Misty slaps him across the chest and he flinches. "What?! Am I wrong for saying we shouldn't be standing around a dead body?"

"All right," I say to him. "Keep your panties on. We're leaving."

***

Lillian and her two guys are waiting for us in the foyer when we come up from the basement. As soon as she sees us, she stands up, the color coming back into her face. "Thank goodness," she says. "I was about to come find you guys."

"We thought we heard shots," says one of her men. "Is everybody whole?"

"Yeah," I answer. "We need to haul ass though. I'll explain on the way."

Lillian nods, her eyes drifting over to Eris. "She coming with us?"

"Yes," I say to her. "She's one of us."

To my surprise, Lillian smiles at that and says to her, "Welcome to the family."

"Mac, I need a couple of things," Eris says.

I squint my eyes at her and say, "Three minutes. We'll be waiting outside. Misty, go with her and help."

***

Eris and Misty run up to her bedroom while the rest of us leave the house and load up in the van. It's still broad-ass daylight. I have no doubt when they find Randall Loving's body they'll have our faces all over the net before sundown. Ah well. They've been collectively trying to catch us for years. Nothing new there.

I grin as Eris and Misty join us in the van, literally in three minutes. "Learned to tell time, I see," I say softly to Eris.

She gently punches my good arm and we share a quiet chuckle.

The drive back is easier than the drive-in. They don't stop us at the gates. We get a mile or so away from the central hub before Lillian points to my backpack. "What are you going to do with the scepter?"

I'd forgotten about it. Its value is kind of useless to me now. We know the truth, the real truth, about Magnus Circadia. I pull the scepter out of the bag. It's just a hunk of decorative metal infused with trace amounts of mage poison.

"I don't know," I say with a sigh. I look at Eris. "It's your family's history in more ways than one. Maybe you should decide."

She scrunches her nose up at it. "Yeah, I don't think so. That thing has caused too much trouble for both our families."

I nod and keep thinking. Then it hits me. I lean over and yell out to Misty, "Drive by the bay for a second."

Misty turns the van around and we're driving towards the bay nearby. It's a small docking area next to Lake Orton. The lake goes out for a few miles before turning into a stream that eventually leads to the ocean. It's a longer drive to the ocean, though, so this will have to do.

She pulls up to the dock. I get out of the van, scepter in hand. As I walk, I hear Eris running up behind me. She takes my hand as we walk along the wooden boards.

"It's so beautiful out here," she says, looking out at the muddy lake and the low green hills and small trees on the shore. I snicker. "You really don't get out much, do you?"

She laughs. "I guess that's about to change."

"You bet." We reach the end of the dock and take in the quiet of the moment. There's nothing but the sound of the water lapping against the dock posts beneath us...

I feel her hand squeeze mine. "I love you, Mac," she says softly.

"Love you, too, Princess."

She laughs and leans her head against my arm. "Time to begin at the beginning."

"Yup." I hold the scepter in one hand, getting a good grip on it, and then I throw it, letting it sail out and over the water. It goes far, glinting silver end over end until it splashes near the center of the lake.

"Let's begin at the beginning."

EPILOGUE

· · · ● · ● · ● · · ·

ONE YEAR AND THREE months, almost to the day, since my emancipation. It annoys Mac when I call it that. He says it's corny. I always say that if he knows a better word, I'd love to hear it.

I'm looking at my dress in the mirror. Gold lace, white silk, form-fitting over my hips and flaring out at the bottom. Lillian had one of her people make this for me to my specifications and I look amazing in it.

I am nervous and not sure why. I love Mac. He's the only man I want to be with, who I've ever wanted to be with. So, why is my stomach in knots?

Maybe because my mom is here. Nobody was more surprised than me when she walked into Josie's diner looking for a shifter who would deliver a letter to me. We've cautiously rebuilt our relationship over the past year. I don't know if I can ever completely forgive her for the part she played, I love her. She's the only mother I've known and I've come to appreciate family more than I ever thought I could. The security hoops she had to go through to be here today would be comical if it wasn't deadly serious and necessary.

My dress is off the shoulder, showing off the dulled lines from where Mac marked me. I'm looking at it in the mirror, my finger tracing the jagged lines. I feel like I was his the moment he marked me. This wedding business is just a technicality.

I take a deep breath and say aloud, "It's gonna be okay. It's gonna be okay."

I walk away from the mirror. Mac's best friend Dire was kind enough to allow us to stay in one of their cabins in this mystical paradise they live in. I look out of the window and see hills and hills of green-capped by red and gold sunlight rising above the trees of the forest. This place is so beautiful. And apparently, no one but Mac's friend Dire and his wife even know where it is or how to get to it. We had to be portalled here by Dire.

There's a knock at the door. "Come in." Lillian pokes her head in. She smiles, her eyes going to my dress.

"Mind if we come in?"

"Who's we?"

She walks in with Aliyah, Dire's wife. "You look beautiful," she says as she walks in.

"Thank you. It really turned out good, didn't it?"

She nods and Lillian says, "It did. Mac's going to be wowed when he sees you."

"I hope so. I really hope so."

They exchange glances, and then Aliyah says, "Lillian, please make sure that everything's ready for me."

"Of course." She pauses and steps between us to give me a kiss on the cheek, then she leaves.

And I'm here with Aliyah. The way everyone has talked about her all this time, you'd think she was the queen of the bikers. "May I add something to your dress?"

"Sure?"

She raises a hand and a cloud of golden glitter floats from her fingertips to my dress and my arms, showering me in a soft, golden glow.

"Now, you're perfect," she says.

"Thank you." I feel so honored. I think about how she and Dire got together and how she has chosen a similar path to mine. She sacrificed her entire life like I have.

"Can I ask you something?"

"Sure," she says.

"Is it worth it? All of this? Being with men like Mac and Dire? Is it worth it?"

Her gentle face splits into an easy smile. "Oh, yes," she says. "Every minute of it."

"You make it sound so good."

Aliyah sighs and takes my hand, walking over to the mirror. "It's funny how now feels like the moment of truth," she says as she looks at me in the mirror, adjusting the veil folded into my curls. "But...you probably already know where you belong, don't you?"

Her fingers touch the mark on my shoulder, and I chuckle. "Yeah, I guess so. I just…I want this to go perfectly. I want a perfect life with Mac."

"You should know by now that nothing's perfect," she says. "All that matters is for the two of you to be together. There's nothing you can't conquer together."

I like how she put that. I wonder so much about the struggles she and Dire must have seen. She makes it look easy. I hope I can be like her when Mac and I have been together for a while.

Another knock. This time, they don't wait for us before opening the door. It's Misty. She's got Aaron, Dire and Aliyah's son, on her hip. He's an adorable toddler. Smooth dark skin like his father's and a mass of curly dark hair. "Sorry," she says, "But Dire wanted me to let you know we're about ready to start."

"All right," I say. "We're coming."

I take another final look in the mirror and Aliyah pats me on the back. "Time to jump in."

I laugh. "With both feet."

We walk out of the room together, through the cabin, and out into the field behind the house. Into the sunlight. Our friends and family are gathered in a circle, as is the tradition. Mac is in the center. His eyes widen the second he sees me, and I feel like I can fly.

I walk to him, my eyes and his are connected. There's no one but us, each for the other. He takes my hands as I stop before him, and whispers, "You...you look like...like a princess."

I bust out with a delighted laugh and he joins in.

Raising my hand to his face, I say, "I guess that makes you my prince."

"I guess so. Forever and ever?"

"Forever and ever."